HEART WARD

An Inner Origins Companion Book

ELLIS LOGAN

An Earth Lodge® Publication
Roxbury, Connecticut

Published in the U.S.A. by Earth Lodge®
Cover Design by Maya Cointreau

ISBN 978-1-944396-31-2

More Books in the Inner Origins Series

Shades of Valhalla

Fates of Midgard

Gifts of Elysielle

"Hear my soul speak.
Of the very instant that I saw you,
Did my heart fly at your service."

Shakespeare
The Tempest

PROLOGUE

I should have listened.

I should have stayed outside.

But the sound of silence was overwhelming. A mail courier walked by on the brownstone-lined street, yet I barely heard her steps through the hush of the trees, the absence of the birds. I felt frozen, weighed down under the watchful eyes of the squirrels, unmoving on their branches.

I'd never sensed such stillness and burden in the air.

When a gust of wind blasted me without warning, it shocked me, raw against my skin, and I couldn't help it.

I turned and ran, in through the door hanging precariously on broken hinges, past the shoes of all sizes lined up haphazardly in the hall, into the living room.

At first, I thought maybe there had been an accident with some paint. A home decorating project gone awry.

But then, I saw the hand on the coffee table, severed fingers lined up so neatly, so carefully nearby. Hair in clumps, strewn about the floor, on the couches, on the-

Suddenly, the world was quiet no more. A high-pitched noise filled all my senses, piercing my ears. I closed my eyes against the sound and fell to my knees, clapping my hands over my ears. Trying to make it stop. Trying to shut out what I had seen.

But it was too late.

The piercing sound continued to build, and I knew I would never, ever be able to silence it. Because it was me. It was the sound of the person I'd been shattering, of something fragile inside me ripping apart into a thousand brittle pieces.

I was the one screaming. And nothing would ever be the same.

CHAPTER 1

I couldn't remember my last full night of sleep. I was investigating yet another financial firm in downtown Manhattan when the call came in, robbing me of any hope that tonight would be any different.

"Ward," I'd answered. Dressed in a custodial outfit and carrying a bottle of glass cleaner, cloth chamois sticking out of my back pocket, no one gave me second glance as I weaved through the cubicles. This late at night, only grunts and lackeys were working, too busy trying to make a good impression on their bosses to care about someone like me.

"Situation report?" the cool voice came over the line, laced with the static of a bad connection.

"Clean."

A frustrated sigh broadcasted clearly. "Dammit. The Morrigan's got everyone tightening their nets."

"I know. Everything's been wiped here." We'd been searching for a paper trail to the research facilities of the Morrigan for months, and still had nothing to show for it. The leader of the Shades had been attacking our people with some sort of anti-serum that threw Light fae into comas, and our scientists had no idea how to counteract it. We needed to find a cure, and we needed it yesterday. The medical facilities in Valhalla were starting to fill up, and everyone was worrying about what would happen if Mikael Morrigan decided to escalate and do something on a larger scale.

It wasn't really a question of if, but when.

"Just as well, I suppose. Amber and Ewan have reported in, they're on a flight back from Vancouver getting in later tonight. I'm going to need you to stop on your way back north to pick someone up at Vala's and bring them in." Mitch Slaight's voice faded in and out, and I wasn't sure I heard him right.

"Did you say you want me to stop at Vala's? Sorry, this connection is pretty crappy."

"Yeah, a faeling seems to have gotten herself in trouble with the Shades. They took the girl's mother, but she managed to get away somehow. Find a place to lie low overnight and get there as early as you can in the morning to pick her up."

"You want me to bring some kid all the way up to Montreal on my bike? I don't know, isn't that illegal or something?" I put the glass cleaner down on a desk as I walked and ran a hand through my hair, considering.

"No, not a kid. A teenager. Vala says she has all her papers, so crossing the border should be no problem. Just start making your way up to Vermont, get some rest, and get her to the safehouse in one piece. She might have intel that can help us."

4

"Not holding my breath here," I snorted.

A frazzled looking brunette looked up from her computer screen and gave me the once over. Her mouth opened just a little and her eyes widened in appreciation, following me as I passed. If I'd had some time to kill, maybe I would have taken her up on the invitation clear in her eyes. She might be working in a banking firm with Dark affiliations, but chances were she was just another clueless human. Still, maybe I could come back another time and see if I could hit her up for some information. Sometimes, it was the people lowest on the ladder who noticed things, simply because they were motivated enough, or jealous enough, to pay attention. But, duty called. No time for fun. I winked at her and headed out of the office to the elevators.

"Look, Alec, this girl, she's a V.I.P., make sure you treat her like one." I rolled my eyes, barely listening. "You've met her mother, Frederika Alvarsson."

"Fred?" The name snapped me back to attention. "I didn't know she had a daughter." I'd attended several training seminars with Frederika Alvarsson, learning human fighting techniques like Krav Maga and Aikido. She'd made a big impression on me each time, with her easy manner, big smile, and hard-hitting punches. I'd learned a lot from her.

"Vala thinks this girl is important, so until we know otherwise, we treat her that way."

I grunted impatiently. It didn't really matter either way to me. I just wanted to get on the road, sleep in my own bed. "Right, and we know Vala's never wrong."

"Not often enough for anyone to remember, anyway. So you get that girl here in one piece."

The elevator dinged its arrival.

"Okay, ride's here. I'm going to lose you in a minute. Don't worry about the girl, I'll protect her with my life, whoever she is."

"I know you will, Ward, that's why I called you. I have some things to take care of here in Chicago, but I'll be back up to Montreal the day after tomorrow. We can talk more then."

Mitch hung up and the line went dead, just as the elevator started descending.

"Nice talking to you, too," I said, sticking the phone back in my pocket. I rode down to the building's underground garage without incident and walked over to my motorcycle. Well, okay, it wasn't my bike, not really. It belonged to the Light Guard, just like the safehouse and most of the furnishings associated with it. After all, Light fae operated on a fairly socialistic model, providing for everyone's needs and sharing as needed. But Mitch had let me pick out the bike myself, and no one else rode it. Ever.

I smoothed my hand over the smooth matte black paint, taking a moment to appreciate the naked beauty of the all-terrain Ducati Monster. I didn't have much to call my own, had never really wanted a home or a family, not since I was a young kid, so the bike was about as close as I ever expected to come to true love.

A bike would never let you down. A bike would never leave you. And, instead of making promises she couldn't keep, she purred like a tiger.

I ditched my lightweight coveralls, stuffed them behind a nearby support column and opened the small storage hatch on the front of the bike where I always kept an extra helmet and travel essentials like toothpaste and clean t-shirts. I'd learned the hard way that it paid to always be prepared. Plus, chicks dug it when I pulled the gentleman card and handed them the spare headgear, caring about their safety and all that.

I put my phone and wallet inside the compartment, climbed on the bike and gunned the engine. Pulling out of my parking space, I made my way through the garage feeling resigned. Normally I loved visiting Vala, but this time it was as appealing as a bowl full of Brussels sprouts. As much as I liked Frederika, the word V.I.P. had put me on edge. I didn't have time for some snotty over-privileged faeling and her drama. We had real problems on our hands, and it wasn't like the Dark were going to call a time-out. Not that anyone would ask my opinion on the matter.

Still, Frederika was a friend, and I really respected her as a Guardian, one of the Light fae who watched over the human world above Aeden. If she was in trouble with the Shades, then I owed it to her to take good care of her kid.

I left the garage, flashing my comped parking pass as I left, and pressed play on the helmet's micro-radio. The furious flute solo of Jethro Tull's "Locomotive Breath" washed over me, picking up where it had left off a couple hour ago. I took a deep breath, readying myself, and blasted out into downtown traffic, the bike sounding its own roar of approval.

Time to go meet the princess.

CHAPTER 2

Six hours in the Comfort Motel outside Albany had been anything but. The drive out of Manhattan had sucked, hitting accident after accident and having to evade more than one oblivious driver switching lanes without checking their mirrors. Still, six hours of crappy sleep were better than no sleep at all. The coffee in the lobby at 7:30am wasn't any better than my room had been, but at least it burned the haze from my eyes.

I settled my tab and hit the road again. GPS had Vala's at two hours from Albany – I made it there in an hour thirty, listening to a Nu Jazz playlist my friend Amber had made in an attempt to lure me to the darker side of techno.

I sped along the dirt track that led to Vala's, a nearly invisible pass through the woods, but slowed down as I neared the house. The Druid would kill me if I tore through her gravel parking area.

I parked near the fountain next to some beat to hell pickup truck and yanked my helmet off my head. Trying to delay the inevitable, I cracked my neck a couple of times. I generally tried to avoid kids as much as possible. Boys were loud, and they asked too many questions. Girls...Well, they just tended to remind me of my sister. Teens weren't any better. Farrah would have been nineteen this year, still a teen herself.

"You going to just stand there all day, or you gonna come over here and give me a hug?" The warm rich voice poured over me like honey.

"Vala, sweetheart," I walked up the stairs to the house and wrapped her ample frame in my arms. "It's good to see you."

"So, Bran sent you, did he?" Her eyes twinkled, as if there was a secret buried behind the chocolate velvet orbs.

"Were you expecting someone else?"

She laughed, a deep throaty sound. "Not at all, dear boy. Just enjoy watching life unfold, that is all. Like I said, it's good to see you."

"So, I hear Frederika Alvarsson's gotten herself into some trouble, and her daughter needs sanctuary?"

"Oh, it goes much, much deeper than that. Siri's got something special in her, still not sure how it's all going to work out, but I think she might be just the thing you all have been looking for."

"What do you mean?"

"You'll see, soon enough. In fact, why don't you go and see if you can round her and her friend up, while I finish making breakfast. Can't send you two off without a proper meal." She looked me up and down. "Aren't they feeding you, boy? You've lost weight since the last time you were here. Not that it doesn't suit you, but still."

"It's hard to eat well when you're running missions seven days a week. And no one could ever feed me as well as you do."

I'd known Vala for years, ever since I'd joined the Light Guard and started running missions in Midgard, out on the surface of the Earth above Aeden. Officially, Vala was sworn to remain neutral in fae matters, lending her seer capabilities as a Druid to both Light and Dark. In reality, she had a soft spot for the Light, since our side protected nature, just like the Druids. Myself, I loved her cooking and her warm hugs. If I was honest with myself, she was the closest I had had to a mom since my father had taken me below to live with our people in Aeden.

Vala was like family. Anytime I could find a reason to stop in, I did. Still, that glitter in her eyes put me on alert. She was hiding something from me, something she'd seen, or heard. But what?

"You said the girl has a friend with her. Are they in danger, too?"

"Rowan? No, he'll be fine, he's in no danger at all. Sweet faeling. He's the one who thought to bring Siri here. That's his truck behind you."

"Okay." Whatever Vala's secret was, she wasn't going to spill anytime soon. I sighed, and resigned myself to playing the Druid's game. "So, out back, you said?"

"Yes, last I checked, Rowan was waiting for Siri to come back from her morning run in the woods. She's an earth fae, like you. I think the forest helps her feel more at ease." She ushered me into the house and shooed me down the hall. "Now get, I'll call you in when food's on."

I walked through the old colonial house, trailing my hand absently along the gleaming wooden tables, smiling at the cacophony of Native American hand drums mixed in with Celtic knot work and massive crystals perched precariously on ledges. I pushed through the back door and stopped. Two teens were sparring on the lawn. Not kids at all, faelings of Choosing age. I caught the door just before it was about to slam shut, instinct making me dull the noise.

The boy wasn't bad. Rough movements, but clearly some training. He needed more work, for sure, but he'd be able to hold his own in a bar fight.

Too bad he was fighting a professional.

CHAPTER 3

The girl was obviously Fred's daughter. She flowed with the same economy of movement, the same grace. I leaned against the door, enjoying what I was seeing. She was playing to his ego, taking it easy on him, allowing him to feel like he had a chance at beating her. It was cute. High-school, but cute. And the kind of thing that would get your butt kicked in Guard training.

Her legs were toned under tight workout pants, her arms sinewy and muscled in an old grey tee shirt. Her warm blonde hair was in two long, messy braids that flew as she twirled, moving effortlessly from a Tang Soo Do strike into a complicated Capoeira form, cartwheeling around her partner to knock him back a few feet with a macaco roundoff ending in a kick to his shoulder.

She laughed, clearly enjoying herself, and I couldn't help grinning in response. Fred had probably started training the girl as soon as she could walk. The guy didn't stand a chance. Even as he stepped up his attack, wrapping her in his arms, that much was clear.

Seconds later, the kid was on the ground. The girl hadn't pulled any of her punches, using some fierce Krav Maga moves to lay him up. The guy was going to have bruises come nightfall, if they weren't forming already. He knew he was beat, too, and threw his arms out wide across the grass in classic surrender.

I had to work to keep from laughing, and clapped instead, definitely having enjoyed the show. I forgot to take the girl's recent brush with the Shades into account – you could practically see her hackles raise when she realized someone had been watching them and she dropped down into a defensive stance without thinking.

She looked up at me, an angry scowl on her face. I couldn't help it. It was like being growled at by a puppy. Something about her was so innocent, so fresh, the glare surprised me and I laughed. Her eyes narrowed and I figured a compliment might smooth things over.

"That was awesome!" I clapped a few more times. "I don't think I've seen anyone get owned like that in at least a year." The boy didn't think I was funny, apparently, and growled as he staggered back to his feet.

"Can we help you?" the girl demanded coldly.

"On the contrary," I said, pushing away from the building and walking down the steps, moving slowly so as not to frighten her. "I believe I am here to help you." I smiled at her as I approached, figuring that ought to help her see I was a friend and not foe.

"Really?" the friend drawled. "And how could you possibly help us? Vala sent for a trained Light Guard. You want us to believe they sent you instead? You don't look any older than us."

The girl watched me come closer through wisps of hair. I couldn't see her eyes clearly, and I felt the strangest urge to push her hair out of her face. Probably not a wise move, I decided, and made my body stay relaxed. She still hadn't dropped her defensive stance.

"He has a point. Show us what you can do," the girl said, stretching out her hand and beckoning me towards her like someone out of an old Kung Fu movie.

This, I could work with. I smiled and launched into some basic lasair, a specialized form of fae martial arts that integrated dancelike moves and acrobatics in a way that made Brazilian capoeira look positively remedial. The word itself meant "flash of light," which is exactly what the fleeting moves would look like if your brain could process what was happening before you were taken down.

I went easy on her, making sure I didn't throw her anything she couldn't handle. Then, I decided *what the hell*, and grabbed her from behind in a classic old-Norse wrestling move straight out of a glima handbook. Moments later, she was flat on her back, pinned under me while I straddled her hips.

She struggled, and I realized I still couldn't see her eyes. Without even making a conscious decision to do it, I called up my earth power and thin, strong vines slithered out from the ground, wrapping around her, holding her still. One vine brushed her hair away from her face and she looked up, locking eyes with me.

Silver. Liquid mercury. Grey just a touch clearer than my mom's. Like my sister's. Memories rocked through me, making me go cold for a moment. She began to struggle again, glaring at me and looking at the vines that held her as if she could burn them off with laser vision. I left my hands on her shoulders and felt thankful she wasn't a fire fae.

"Let. Me. Go."

"Not until you concede defeat." I smiled calmly, assuming the role of teacher again.

"Clearly, you win," she ground out.

I stood up and looked at her. She'd conceded, but without any sort of grace. A good instructor made difficult students work for an end to their lesson. Plus, I was enjoying the flush creeping up her skin, betraying her frustration.

"You heard her," the friend stepped towards me, his hands fisting at his sides. "Let her up."

"Ah, are you going to make me?" I looked down at him, amused this guy thought he could take me. "Don't forget, I am already familiar with your fighting style."

The boy didn't back down or back up, which impressed me.

"Just let her up," he repeated.

"I don't think so," I mused, coming to a decision. "I think, we should see what else she can do."

I knelt down next to the girl and put my hand on her arm. Sudden warmth eclipsed everything in my mind and

16

I lost the ability to think. For a moment, I couldn't breathe as sheer joy flashed through me. It felt like a blast of sunshine was riding through my entire body, lighting up every cell, pulling me, pushing me towards her. I could see she felt it too, her eyes wide and gleaming as suddenly she struggled more aggressively against her bonds. I'd never felt anything like it before, not once among a thousand touches from other Light fae, and I knew it in an instant for what it was.

A myth. A fairy tale.

The surge.

A connection between two people that went beyond love, beyond duty. A complete connection of bodies, minds, spirits. At least, that's what people said. Most people didn't believe in it. I certainly never had. I didn't.

No.

I snatched my hand back, deciding it had to be something else, some kind of trick.

"Who are you?" I demanded.

"Who am I? Who the hell are you?" she retorted. "And when are you going to let me up?"

"Right, sorry." I shrugged, trying to shake off whatever had just happened. "I wanted to see if you could do it yourself. Vala said you were showing Earth powers. Is that true?"

Teacher. Be a teacher, I thought, pushing all thoughts of the surge from my mind. For gods' sakes, this was Fred Alvarsson's daughter. I had to get a grip.

"Um, yes, I think so. I mean, that's what everybody says."

"Okay, so let's see if you can do this. I need to you to quiet your mind."

"Easier said than done," she muttered. "Can you, maybe, back up a little bit. You're kind of freaking me out still."

"Okay, sure." I moved back to stand with her friend, who made a point of not looking at me.

"Better?"

She nodded. The flush had started to recede from her skin, and I found myself wanting to bring it back. Focus, Alec, I thought.

"Good. So, now, quiet your mind. Just relax. Take a few deep breaths in and out, and push your energy out to the vines. Thank them and ask them to release you."

At first, nothing happened. But then I detected a faint glow emanating from her head, vibrant yellow rays reached out around her and flowed into the plants surrounding her. I'd been able to see auras for years, but I'd never anything like that. Never in daylight. Never unbidden. The sight stunned me, and I watched as the vines slowly unwound from her body and retreated back into the ground.

"Wow," the boy whispered. "That was so cool."

She kipped up onto her feet and brushed off her pants.

"Thanks." She smiled at her friend and then looked at me. "I didn't know I could do stuff like that. Will I be able to call them up like you did, too?"

"Definitely. I think you'll be able to do that, and a whole lot more," I said, wondering just what I'd gotten myself into. I pushed the thought away and thrust out a hand in greeting. "The name's Alec Ward."

"Siri Alvarsson," she answered, grasping my hand. The surge reared up again, shocking me with its intensity. I felt warmth, a pull to draw her closer, and a taste of her own interest. This was not good. I didn't have room in my life right now for fairy tales. I dropped her hand quickly and turned to her friend. The rush of feelings receded, and I felt cold in their absence.

"And you would be?"

"The boyfriend, Rowan Carey," he said, slapping his hand on mine. Instantly, my stomach lurched and cold, hard ice prickled through my veins. I yanked my hand out of Rowan's grip and moved behind him before either of them could blink, restraining both his arms.

"You're a Shade! Why are you here?"

"Easy dude, Rowan is not a Shade." Siri rushed to my side, putting a hand on my shoulder.

"He is, I sensed it the moment I touched him," I sneered and shrugged off her hand. "He's been lying to you. Besides, he's a Carey. They're all dark."

"Look, Alec, I promise, Rowan is not dark. He hasn't even Chosen yet."

"Get off me, you jerk," Rowan tried to shake me off, and my grip tightened.

"You can't blame him for who his parents are!" Siri yelled.

I stared at her. Was she insane? Didn't she know how dangerous this boy could be?

"Stand down, Ward!" Vala called from one of the windows on the first floor. "The girl is right. He's proven himself trustworthy, so far."

"How do you know it's not a trap?" I called back to her over my shoulder.

"You dare question my judgement? Have you been having your own visions now, Alec?" She chuckled. "Let the poor boy go. If he'd wanted to harm her, he could have handed her over days ago."

I groaned in frustration, shoving Rowan away from myself in disgust. Everyone here was crazy.

The girl hugged Rowan to her for a moment, and I twitched, wanting to yank her out of his arms. How could she stand to hold him? The touch of a Shade, even a young darkling, was never pleasant for a Light fae. He shrugged her off and stalked away into the woods. She started to follow him but Vala called her back, and I exhaled with relief. There was no way I could have allowed her in the woods with him, alone. And I had a feeling the less I saw of him, the better.

"Let him go, child," Vala was telling her. "His pride's been broken. Let him have some time to put it back together."

"Fine," she muttered, kicking at a dandelion. "Miko, can you go with him? I still don't think it's safe for him to be out there alone." I looked around, wondering who she was talking to, but all I saw was a squirrel bounding away through the forest canopy. Surely, she wasn't talking to him. Was she?

"You can talk to the animals?" I asked. I'd thought she was a faeling, but if she had already Chosen... "How long have you been with the Light?"

"I'm not with the Light. I didn't even know I was fae until recently, and I don't turn eighteen until January." She looked at me. "What?"

That wasn't possible. She had to be lying. Or have her birthday wrong. No one got their powers before their Choosing. Some people even had to wait years for them to manifest. And talking to animals was definitely an ability. A rare, Ancient one, at that.

"But then how did you-" I broke off, shook my head and started again. "How long have you been manifesting abilities for?"

"A few weeks. So? I mean, my mom said it was a little early, but it can't be that unusual, can it?"

"It's completely unusual. I don't know anyone who manifested before they turned eighteen, other than the Elders."

"And here I thought my mom was just putting off telling me about this fae stuff because she didn't want to face me getting older." She laughed. "But she really was telling the truth... She really thought she'd have more time..." She trailed off, looking distressed at the thought of her mom. I knew that look. I knew that feeling. Without thinking, I wrapped my arms around her, wanting to protect.

"Hey," I said. "Don't worry about your mother. We're going to figure this all out, I swear. You will have the best resources behind you, and we will find Frederika."

I remembered why I was here, and released her, hoping she wouldn't start crying or anything. I wasn't sure what I'd do if that happened.

"She trained me, you know," I said without meaning to.

She looked at me doubtfully. "Obviously she taught us different things."

"No really, she did. The Guard has their own style of martial fighting, but Frederika leads training seminars every year or so to help catch us up on human fighting techniques. I've taken several of her workshops. It's important for us to know how to deal with any opponent."

"Well, you seem to have it down," she said, seeming annoyed. At least she didn't look like she was going to break down anymore.

Behind her, I saw Rowan creeping back out of the woods, just as Vala called for us all to come in for brunch. I turned and strode back to the house, not bothering to wait for the darkling.

Still, I couldn't help turning to make sure they followed, and caught a glimpse of the boy holding the door closed before Siri could enter, turning to say something to her. Whatever it said, it must have worked, because she smiled up at him and winked. He said something else and she kissed him. Disgusted and feeling like a creepy voyeur, I left them to it and went to the dining room, waiting for them to join us.

CHAPTER 4

I bowed my head, getting ready to say grace.

"We accept this feast today with gratitude to all the beings who contributed to its bounty, the animals and plants, the farmers and the land itself. May it fill our hearts, bodies and minds with the blessings and the radiance of Aeden, aho-em."

Siri stared at me, looking bemused.

"Penny for your thoughts, Siri?" Vala asked as she passed around a huge bowl of Caesar salad.

"I was just thinking back to the last time I heard a fae say grace. Do all fae say grace in Aeden?" She looked at me while she helped herself to a massive helping of fruit salad.

"We all bless our food in pretty much the same way," I said. "When we make our food, we also usually bless and energize it."

"But, well, you talked about thanks and gratitude. The other fae I heard thanked his Lord for dominion over the earth and for his help in seeking the light."

"Dark fae." I snapped as I gripped the salad tongs, incensed that this girl could have shared dinner with an entire family of Shades. What the hell had Frederika been thinking?

"Easy, Alec," Vala cautioned me.

I let up on the tongs, but couldn't help glaring at the boy.

"Okay," Siri continued, "but now I am wondering who is the Lord that they were thanking – was it a deity all the fae worship, or is it someone like Mikael, the man who's currently holding my mom prisoner?" Her friend looked stunned, like he had never thought about it. And he probably hadn't.

"It's just grace, Siri. My dad says the same thing at every meal," the darkling boyfriend complained.

"Yeah, but think about it. It sounds all nice and god-like, but even before I knew Sully was Dark fae the words he used creeped me out a little. I thought you guys were Lutheran or something with all that talk about dominion and toil."

Rowan's face tightened in anger. Showing his true colors, as far as I was concerned.

"Look, I don't want to upset you, I'm just curious, okay?" Siri turned to me, "My mom never said grace, except at Thanksgiving. This is all still so new to me. But it seems obvious now that when his dad spoke about finding the light with the Lord's blessing, he was actually talking about finding Light fae, not radiance like you just talked about. So who is this Lord? Is it a god or a person?"

"As far as I know, no fae believe in any specific god. Not the Dark, and not the Light." I thought about it. When we talked about gods, we were really invoking the power of the elders, the Ancients. How should I explain it in a way she would understand? "We believe in Spirit, a unifying energy behind all existence and matter, and we are able to harness that energy, but any 'Lord' Sullivan mentioned probably had to do with the leader of the Dark fae council. Here in the Americas, that would be Mikael."

I watched the blood drain from her face as I continued. "Every continent has their own council. Each leader of the local council serves on a high council that rules all Shades. There is no one leader of the Shades, they all mistrust each other too much to bow to one leader. Our intel, however, indicates that Mikael would like to change all that."

"And you think my father is helping him with that? You think my family is part of this, that the Shades hunt Light fae for fun?" Rowan demanded, sounding outraged. Maybe he really was as clueless as he pretended.

"Easy Rowan, no one's talking about your family." Siri said, "Alec is just telling me what he knows about the Dark council."

"Actually," I said, thinking of the atrocities I had witnessed, things no person should ever have to see, "the Dark do hunt the light for fun. Every Shade warrior that I've gone up against seems to thoroughly enjoy the pain they inflict on the innocent, whether they are Light fae or just unlucky humans who've gotten in the way. If your father is working with Mikael, then he is directly involved in the hunting of Light fae."

"Alec," Vala shook her head in warned me. "This is not the time."

"Really, Vala, then when is the time? I'm not going to lie to her, and I'm not going to let this darkling get away with believing whatever crap his parents have told him; she asked a question and she deserves an honest answer. The Light does not shield faelings from the truth, no matter how painful or ugly it might be. We give them the benefit of an upbringing steeped in truth and honesty."

I turned on the girl, inflamed. She didn't deserve mercy. The Shades certainly hadn't given my family any. They never did.

"The fae have always been heart-centered, trusting, giving people. The Light fae still hold to those values. We are quick to forgive, and slow to hate." I paused, feeling sorry that I couldn't shield this girl from reality. For a moment, I wanted to do that so badly. I allowed myself to think of a life with a real bonds, with people I cared about, for just a moment. "When love comes, it comes instantly. We hold nothing back."

Her eyes widened, locked on mine. Trusting. Open. I knew that look. Girls gave it to me all the time, and I let them. But not this time. Not with this girl. Not while the Dark continued to pull families apart. Somehow, I knew if I let her in, I'd never get her out.

"The Dark have taken everything that comes naturally to us and distorted it. Where we trust, they take advantage. Where we love, they consume. Where we forgive, they hate and seek revenge. Where we protect, they abuse. Where we value honesty, they lie. Where we seek harmony, they sow discord and lust for power. There is nothing honorable left in the Dark. They have twisted everything that we hold dear. Every Light fae who has ever trusted a Shade has come to regret it. Every. Single. One."

I speared the darkling with a glance, feeling an unwelcome twinge of regret for the boy who'd been unfortunate enough to be born a Carey.

Rowan looked at me with pure hate, his eyes darkening. Proving my point.

"That will never happen." He ground out. "I will never give Siri a reason to regret trusting me. She is everything to me, more important than my family, more important than anything on the planet."

"And that is how you will fail her," I said in a low voice. "No Light fae would ever even think to make such a promise. Nothing is more important than our charge. Nothing is more important than the whole of the planet. It is the core of our soul." I looked back at the girl, driven to explain. "Our love for every facet of the Earth is the same as our love for ourselves, for our mates, for our children. We cannot separate ourselves from that love because it is all of who and what we are. So you see, you can never keep the promises you are making, because the very nature of them betrays you for what you really are."

Rowan looked ready to leap across the table and attack me. Secretly, I found myself hoping he would. Vala distracted us all with a gentle cough, rising from the table.

"Alec, can you grab Siri's plate please? The second course should be ready now." Somehow she managed to sound like nothing out of the ordinary was going on. I followed her into the kitchen, leaving the two friends – or lovers? – alone at the table. I wondered what Rowan would say now, how he would try to deny who and what he was.

"You shouldn't have been so hard on the boy," Vala scolded me as soon as we were out of hearing range. "He's not Dark yet."

"Isn't he? I knew what he was the minute I touched him. The darkness runs through his veins, it's in his skin. How can she stand to be near him?"

"She has a big heart. Big enough to heal the world, I'm betting. She can sense the goodness in him, just like I can. Like you could, if you weren't letting your past do your thinking for you."

I grunted and grabbed the steaming platter of strawberry-stuffed French toast, not willing to get into a discussion about me, or my past.

"Are we done here?" I asked.

She sighed and nodded, picking up a huge decanter of maple syrup as she led the way back into the dining room.

I decided to ignore the rest of them and helped myself to a mountain of French toast, swallowing whatever misgivings I had.

Brunch ended, and it was time for us to go. Siri went upstairs to grab her things, while Rowan and I helped Vala

29

clean up. I washed, Rowan dried, and Vala put things away.

I made sure not to touch him again.

I really needed to get out of here. As soon as we were done I excused myself to go wait outside. Fresh air always seemed to calm me down. Vala said some words to Rowan and followed me out.

"Gods, please, not another lecture. I swear, I'll tone it down from here on out."

"That's not what I want to talk to you about. While Siri was here, I saw things. We saw things."

"We?"

"She's a seer, descended from an Ancient who could see the future. Siri can see it, too, sometimes."

"Jesus. Is there anything she can't do?"

"Yes, as sure as you or I. But she is special, there's no getting around that. That's why Mikael took Frederika. He was after Siri. He wants her for something. Wants her to Choose the Dark. She needs you to protect her."

"Well, that's why I'm here, isn't it? To bring her to Aeden?"

"No, it's more than that. You're here because you are supposed to be. I saw it. She took me into one of her visions, with the Morrigan. He's tapping into her visions somehow, seeing what she's seeing. And then, we saw you."

The hairs on the back of my neck stood up, warning me. "What do you mean, you saw me?"

"Running in the woods, exchanging words. Touches. Laughing."

My mind rejected what she was saying, while my body remembered what it had felt like to have my hands on her body.

"No. I don't believe in fate."

"And yet, here we are." Vala smiled at me, raising her eyebrows. "Don't fight fate. Life goes more easily when you trust the flow."

She reached out and took my hands in hers. "Anyway, who are you to decide? The future will happen, regardless of what you think about it."

I started to protest and she cut me off. "Just make sure you don't do anything you might regret. Treat her as something precious, because she is. I think she might hold the fate of the whole world in her hands, that one. That, and her father will likely skin you alive if you don't."

"Her father?"

She smiled wryly. "I suppose I could be wrong, but really, when was the last time that happened? She's Bran Le Fay's daughter, or I'm the Queen of Sheba."

My heart skipped a beat. "The Commander's daughter? Crap. She really is a princess."

I looked over my shoulder and saw Siri walking towards us, dressed simply in jeans, metallic silver hi-top sneakers and a grey hoodie.

"Close enough, dear boy. So you take care now, you hear?" Vala hugged me and let go.

The girl's squirrel ran past her and hopped up onto the Ducati, preening. Well, how was that going to work? Then she fixed her pack on her shoulders, opened the messenger bag at her hips, rearranging some things, and gestured for him to climb in.

"Okay, we're ready." She smiled bravely at us.

Vala rushed over to her and gave her long hug. Then she backed up and held her hands as she had with me, looking into her eyes. Searching.

"I'm going to be thinking of you Siri, all the time. You stay safe now, and let me know anything I can do to help you. Speak with the trees, the winds and the waters, and they will find a way to get your message to me."

"I will, I-"

She broke off and stared vacantly at Vala.

Seconds ticked by.

"Is she okay?" I asked, and saw that Vala had the same tranced out, slack-jawed expression. Dammit. Another vision?

Then they both blinked, wide eyed and scared. They were back.

"Did you see?" Siri asked.

Vala nodded.

"Yes, I saw. I will make sure that doesn't happen. That was no natural disaster, and I can work with the elementals to ensure that it cannot come to pass. Don't worry. I will protect the people you can't." She reached out and put an arm around Rowan. "We both will. Don't waste a single moment worrying about us."

Rowan looked at them both uncertainly, and I knew just what he was thinking. What had they seen?

"He knows you are coming now. He will strengthen his defenses." Vala warned Siri. She closed her eyes, and breathed deeply. "But he does not know everything. You have more power than he knows."

"You can see that? What else do you see?"

"The winds of time blow and change at a whim. I cannot see everything, but I have faith, and I know that you will prevail. It can't be any other way. You must trust, always. Fear is the one true enemy, it leads to all conflict in the world. It is the root of all evil, not greed. Look closely at what triggers you, personally, and what fear it stems from. True empathy, true light, comes from within by imagining yourself in another's shoes, feeling their pain as your own, their joy as your own. When we face our fears head on, then we can be truly empowered and follow our soul's purpose here on earth. Our hearts open up, our minds become unclouded and we can see our way more clearly. Trust is the key. Hold on to that, and you will be fine."

She looked at me meaningfully, as she pulled Siri into a final embrace, letting me know her speech had not just been for Siri's benefit.

I shook my head at her, rolling my eyes and got on the bike, putting on my leather gloves and pulling out helmets for both of us. Siri climbed on behind me, trying not to get too close, but it was a Ducati Monster, no grip bars, no frills. A naked bike. What could she do? She wrapped a hand loosely around my waist, skimming my abs and my hands jumped, gunning the engine in response. We roared down the driveway and she placed her other hand on my hip after waving goodbye.

"You're going to have to hold on," I shouted over the noise of the engine. I wasn't about to lose her now to a bump in the rough road. I reached down and grabbed her right hand, pulling her closer, wrapping her arm around my waist so that she was pressed up against my back. I took her other hand and guided it to clasp her right arm, holding my hand over hers to make sure she'd stay put when I returned my hand to the handlebars.

Of course, she wouldn't. I'd already seen how stubborn she could be. She started to pull her hands away, so I guided the bike over some small ruts in the dirt road, making the bike shudder and jump.

"I told you, hold on!" I yelled again.

She reached back around quickly and sank into me. Grateful she'd given in, I couldn't help myself from reflexively reaching down to squeeze her hand.

Moments later we peeled out onto the even pavement of a real road, heading north. Heading home.

CHAPTER 5

The whole time we rode, my mind tried to process what Vala had told me. Okay, so the girl wasn't a real princess, not really. Her father wasn't on the Light Council, and we didn't actually have royalty anymore among the fae. But as Light Commander, Bran was one of the most important men in all of Aeden.

And who was I? Just another one of his soldiers. Respected, sure. I was damn good at my job. I'd worked hard to become the perfect warrior, training since I was a child. My father had started me off young, even though he had left Aeden to live above below with my mother, a human. He wanted to make sure I had options, make sure I could be a Light Guard, like he had been. He'd enrolled me in kickboxing classes with friends from school, and taught me glima techniques on the weekends on the great lawns of Boston Common.

For all the good it had done us.

The Dark had tracked down my father, found where we lived. He hadn't been active anymore with the Guard, but the Shades didn't know that. I doubt they would have cared, either way. We'd come home, Dad and me, from fishing all day. I'd been so excited, wanting to show my mom the trout I'd caught. Instead, we'd come home to a broken door. My father had ordered me to stay outside, turning hard and cold in an instant, and left me on the front steps.

The silence had gotten to me, more than anything. So I ran inside the house, looking for comfort. Instead, I found my mother in the living room, dead. Tortured. Dismembered. My sister had been killed, too, just for the fun of it, it seemed. What other reason could there be for ending the life of a seven-year old? The house had been covered in blood. We'd left immediately, going straight to Aeden.

I was ten.

There hadn't been a day of my life since then that wasn't dedicated to making sure no one else ever had to go through what I did.

And now, I was supposed to be protecting this faeling, and instead all I could do was think about how her hand had felt in mine. How the blood had roared through my veins, telling me to make her mine.

Me. A half-human. If she was almost a princess, then I was a second-class citizen, looked down upon by so many of her class. Fae didn't interbreed with humans anymore, at least not fae from Aeden. Interaction of that kind was frowned upon. Humans were considered only slightly better than the Shades, weak puppets led into corruption so easily. Too easily. My half human, half fae eyes, green with their ring of purple around them, were like a badge, branding me for what I was.

Guys like me didn't get girls like her. And if I could? I didn't want it. A girlfriend was just another person that could be taken away. Another person that could be lost. I wouldn't let that happen. Not again. Determined to put it out of my mind once and for all, I turned on my music, trying to drown out the feel of her chest pressed against my spine.

Eventually, I had to stop for gas. I tried to ignore her as she shook out her hair and headed inside the convenience store. Soon, too soon, she came back, wearing gloves now and holding two coffees. She held one out.

"Coffee? I added a touch of sugar and some milk to cool it down, hope you don't mind."

"Thanks," I smiled politely, taking it and gulping some down.

"So, um, how much further do we have to go?"

"We're almost at the Canadian border, and then it's another half hour to Montreal, at least. There's a safe-house there where we can stay overnight. We'll ditch the motorcycle and switch to something more suitable for the terrain we'll be covering. We'll have about half a day's drive tomorrow on some pretty rough roads. Speaking of which, we should get going," I finished the rest of the coffee and chucked it in the trash, holding out my hand to take hers as well.

She took her time drinking down the rest of it, holding my gaze the whole time. Daring me. Taunting me. Making me wait.

I tried not to smile, but her defiance amused me.

"You do realize, don't you, that right now, at this very moment while we stand out here in the open, the leader of all the Shades on the American continent has every Dark fae in the area searching for you?"

Her eyes widened over the rim of her cup, but she didn't stop until it was empty. Only then did she hand me the cup. I tossed it over my shoulder into the garbage, raising one eyebrow.

"Sorry," she shrugged. "I'm trying to exercise my trust, since I've been told that fear is my only true enemy."

I snorted. "Trust and faith are all well and good, but believe me, we'd rather not get caught out here alone with the Dark. I'll feel a lot more comfortable when we get to Montreal. There are more of us at the safe-house, and very few Dark live that far north."

"Hey, I can take care of myself you know."

"Really? Like you took care of yourself back there at Vala's?" She really had no idea what we were up against. "Do you want to try again, maybe prove to me just how well you can take of yourself?"

She swallowed, but stood her ground "I'm not afraid of you. Even if you can take me down, you don't scare me."

I took another step closer, coming toe to toe with her. "Well, you scare the hell outta me," I muttered. "C'mon. Time to go."

Back on the bike, I rode as if I could somehow get away from her, away from the temptation, faster than I usually drove. We passed through the border without incident, and arrived in Montreal in the late afternoon.

We drove through the neighborhood of the safehouse, streets lined with brightly painted Victorian row houses, pulling into the alley next to our place to park in a small underground garage. Amber's flashier Ducati was there alongside Ewan's ancient yellow and white International Scout.

Home, or at least the closest thing to it lately.

I walked up the steps to the first floor, letting Siri take her time to follow. Amber's mind-numbing house music was playing above, and I could hear her laughing.

The door at the top of the stair flung open before I got there, and a slight Asian girl stood there with her hand on her hip.

"About time! What'd you do, stop for lunch?" Amber eyed the newcomer over my shoulder. "This the girl?"

"Yeah, we had brunch at Vala's."

Amber moaned and muttered "Lucky" under her breath.

"Siri, this is Amber Slaight. Amber, Siri Alvarsson."

She backed up to let us into walked into the sunlit room decorated in brilliant, functional white with green accents. As usual, everything gleamed, with Amber standing in stark contrast to the room, clad entirely in black, from her platform Docs and tight leather pants to the off the shoulder sweatshirt and heavy emo eyeliner rimming her deep brown eyes. Her long black hair was up in high pigtails streaked with deep purple. I never should have given her those manga comics five years ago.

Nodding toward my friend in torn jeans, work boots and blue flannel lying on the couch, I introduced Siri.

"That big oaf over there's Ewan Patterson. Dude, get your shoes off the couch, you know Mitch'll have your head if he sees you."

"Och, serves him right, outfittin' this place all in white. What does he think this is, the damn Ritz or somethin'?"

"Not everyone has your taste for corduroy and flannel, Ewan." Amber flounced over to a chair nearby and flopped down.

Thirsty, I walked over to the huge glass refrigerator and took out two bottles of flavored seltzer, tossing one to Siri. She took off her bags and sat on the couch next to me. The squirrel crawled out and yawned.

"Sure," Siri cocked her head at Miko and then looked at me. "Is it okay if I get some water for Miko?"

"Oh, yeah, I forgot he was even with you. What does he want, is a bowl good?"

Miko chittered excitedly and she translated, "No, just run the tap for him. He says he'd like to wash up a bit, too."

I nodded and went over to the sink, turning on a thin stream of water. I watched while Miko jumped into the sink, using his hands to cup water to his mouth, and then carefully washed his arms and face in the stream. When he was finished, he hopped up on the counter and set himself to the task of grooming his fur. I turned off the tap, poured out some trail mix as an afterthought and rejoined the group.

"Okay, so just to clarify – did you just have a conversation with that squirrel?" Amber leaned forward on her knees.

"Who, Miko? Sure. Can you understand him?"

"No, of course not. Even in Aeden there are only a handful of fae who can talk with the animals. Well, other than the Ancients, of course." She looked at Siri thoughtfully.

"My mom told me not too many fae can talk with animals, but I wouldn't really know. Miko says that he can hear what any animal or person in thinking, though."

"Really?" Ewan sat up a bit so he could see her better. "Is he some kind of special squirrel?"

Miko snorted loudly and started chattering again.

"Oh, yeah right." She answered Miko and turned back to Ewan. "He says he's not special, that all animals can hear other animals' thoughts. It's just the humans and the fae who have interbred with them that have lost that ability. He calls it animal-speak. Oh, and he wants you all to know that he is my personal guardian for the next eleven months, so not to get any ideas about leaving him behind when I go to Aeden."

"I'm sorry, what?" Was she serious? The squirrel was her guardian? What the hell did that make me? All of us?

She sighed. "It's kind of a long story, but a few weeks ago, I was driving behind this huge truck near Mount Snow and saw it swerve in the road to hit Miko. I actually think it might have been Sullivan Carey driving, but I'm not sure. Anyway, I felt really bad and stopped to see how badly the squirrel was hurt. He was unconscious and I held him for a while... Miko actually says he was almost dead but somehow I healed him or something and after a while he ran away fine. A couple weeks later he showed up near my house, and he's the one who distracted the Shades who busted into our house so I could get away. Now he says he owes me a year of service, some sort of squirrel code of honor or something."

"Wait, so you can talk to animals, and you have healing abilities?" Amber clapped her hands and bounced up and down in her seat, while I rocked back in my seat, stunned. "So it's true then. You really are Bran's daughter."

"Um, I guess? Vala said that was my dad's name. My mom never knew who my dad was, they met on a military mission and they all had code names, so...What?"

All three of us were staring at her in shock. Could Fred really not have had any idea?

I recovered first. "Sorry, it's just-"

"Every fae in Aeden knows who Bran Le Fay is," Amber interrupted. "You're telling me your mom didn't recognize him?"

I glared at Amber, coming to Siri's defense. "Jade raised Fred here, above below, remember? Without knowing his name, how would she have known? Fred never comes to Aeden, I don't know if she ever has."

"Why would my grandmother have kept her out of Aeden?"

"Most fae stay above below, or in Aeden. The only ones who regularly travel back and forth are fae like us," I gestured to Ewan and Amber.

"Fae like you?"

"Light Guards," Ewan yawned.

"But, my mom said that she was a guardian, too. That our whole family stayed here to guard the earth from the Dark."

"She's a guardian. We are Light Guard. Big difference." Amber sank back into her chair again. "The Light Guard is the elite of all the guardians. We keep Aeden safe against unwelcome intruders, and we protect the Light council. We are Aeden's first line defense. I guess you could call us the fae Marines, you know, the best of the best. Hooo yah!" She pumped her fist and laughed at her own antics. "Guardians are skilled, too, don't get me wrong, but they focus more on the day-to-day livelihood of the humans and animals above below than we do."

"Okay, so then you're saying Bran is what, a Light Guard?"

"As if! Bran Le Fay isn't a Light Guard, he's one of the most powerful a-"

"Amber, now is not the time," I interrupted her. I turned to Siri. "Look, I'm sorry, I know you have questions, but your dad, he asked us to just focus on getting you back safely, and leave any debriefing to him. He wants a chance to explain everything to you himself."

She folded my arms over my chest, fire in her eyes. "Oh really, you guys talked about this? You think it's your right to keep me in the dark more than I have been already? Fine. Keep your little fae secrets. Whatever." She jumped up and started pacing.

"You know, you think this is easy for me? You think I give a crap about who my dad might be?" she ranted and my heart beat like a drum in response. Answering her. Cheering her on. "My mom is missing. Missing! Probably being tortured and abused by some Dark psychopath as we speak, and where has he been all these years? I never asked for any of this, I never even had any inkling about this whole, above below bull you guys are talking about. Light fae, Dark fae, Shades, Druid seers. Ugh! I suppose next maybe we can go fight some witches and vampires or something?"

"Actually," Ewan drawled, "most witches are just watered-down fae human hybrids. Of course, there are the Druids, but they are pretty much just humans with heightened senses of telepathy and divination."

She glared at him. "Gee, thanks, I feel so much better now."

"No sweat. Vampires, now that's a different story, those stories all stem from the way the Dark can use their energetic connections to drain life force from humans. And werewolves are just a branch of fae who can shift, too."

"Right, like Fenrir. Miko told me about him." She sighed and sat down on the arm of Ewan's couch. "So, you really think this Bran guy is my dad? I know, I know, you can't tell me about him. Can you at least tell me if he's going to be able to help us, I mean, help me and my mom?"

Ewan reach up and placed a hand on her arm, smiling kindly. "Don't worry, little girl. We will all be helpin' you. Bran will make sure of it. You'll see, he is the best help you could have hoped for."

"Little girl, are you kidding me? What are you, twenty two?"

Ewan laughed, rubbing his hand up and down her arm and she sort of leaned into it, looking more relaxed. I knew it was just a normal reaction to being touched by any Light fae, that warm glow of Light energy that naturally flowed between all of us. I knew Ewan wasn't interested in her. But so help me, if he didn't get his hand off her soon, I might have to do it for him. She looked over at me and I felt my jaw begin to twitch, the way it always did when I was agitated, and tried to tamp the odd feelings down.

Ewan's deep voice pulled her attention back to him. "Sorry, force of habit. You remind me of my youngest sister back home, she's sixteen. But to answer your question, I'm thirty four, and six foot five, both of which pretty much qualify you as little in my eyes, sorry. You want to talk to a twenty two year old, go bug the young twig over there." He pointed at me, still trying to get a grip on my emotions and keep my face from betraying how I was feeling.

She smiled back down at Ewan and I had to take a deep breath. "Okay, Redwood. You got it," she teased.

"Ha, nice one. Redwood, old and tall. I like it." Amber laughed and wiggled her eyebrows, making Ewan and Siri join in. I grimaced and got up, not able to take anymore.

"Come on, I'll show you where you'll be staying tonight."

She shrugged and followed me to the end of the hall where I opened a door, revealing a deep green room with a plush navy blue rug. My room. So much for that good night's sleep I'd been looking forward to. The dark wooden bed had a canopy over it draped with a simple fabric that evoked the night sky and the bed was made, for once. My favorite guitars leaned in the corner next to a pile of books on the floor by the bed. Otherwise, the room was relatively uncluttered. I could have had her bunk in Amber's room, but something made me want her in here, even if I couldn't be with her.

"Wow, this is great. Thanks." She sat down on the edge of the bed and bounced a little, testing it out. "Oh, yeah. This is perfect."

I watched her, giving up all hope of being able to sleep well tonight.

"Right. Well. I'll just leave you to freshen up then. Feel free to take a nap if you want, you must be tired after the long ride. Dinner isn't for a couple hours."

I closed the door behind her and listened to her groan in pleasure, most likely enjoying the comforts of *my* heavenly soft bed. Briefly, I wondered what it would take to make her moan like that in my arms, before I remembered whose daughter she was. I swore softly and beat a hasty retreat to the easy conversation of my fellow Light Guards.

CHAPTER 6

I spent the rest of the day chilling on the couch with my friends, enjoying the novelty of having a day off. It couldn't last forever, of course. Not with Amber around. As soon as the sky darkened, she started on about taking Siri clubbing.

I frowned.

"No way. Not a chance. We're supposed to be protecting her, not taking her to a fae hotspot."

"Aw, come on, Alec, don't be such a stick in the mud." She twirled one of her long pigtails around a finger and made eyes at me. "Please?"

I sighed.

"Might as well give it up now, mate." Ewan chuckled. "You know what she's like."

"Forget it. That Xbox has been calling my name all week. We're staying in. But, to make up for it, dinner's on me."

So that's how it happened. Amber sent us out around 10pm to get poutine, the Montreal specialty of fries smothered in fresh curd cheese and rich beef gravy while Amber attempted to get Sleeping Beauty up.

The whole time we were out, I felt uneasy, like I shouldn't have left the apartment. Left her.

But that was stupid. Amber was a trained Light Guard, and it was the safehouse. As in safe. Warded against the Dark, and owned by shell corporations, untraceable back to the Light.

Ewan didn't seem to notice my mood, never being much for conversation anyway.

When we got back to the flat, the girls greeted us dressed for a night out. Amber hadn't changed much, just put on taller platform shoes and a shorter than short skirt, but she had clearly played dress up and used Siri as the doll. Long, trim legs in skin-tight gunmetal vinyl pants and a silky green top under one of Amber's many quintessential black motorcycle jackets. At least she'd left Siri her shoes, the silver sneakers pairing naturally with what she was wearing.

It didn't matter how hot she looked. She was off-limits and I'd already said we were staying in. As team leader on this one, it was my call, right? I decided to stick with the plan and just ignore whatever *this* was. I dumped the food on the table and got down to the business of eating.

Then, Amber started hounding me about going out.

"Come on, I know you guys said you were just going to hang out and play Skyrim," she rolled her eyes at the mere thought of playing a video game instead of dancing, "but you really owe Siri a good night on the town."

Ewan huffed and went over to the Xbox, clearly determined to ignore her. God, I loved that guy. But I could see Amber wasn't going to give up the fight and caved.

"Fine, we're in. I'll just go change. Come on, Ewan."

"What? Aw, come on, you promised." It was funny to see the great oaf reduced to whining. He followed me reluctantly down the hall, grumbling all the way.

When we returned we allowed Amber to circle us. We'd learned long ago that Amber held final approval on our social acceptability, not us.

"Not bad," she told Ewan, eyeing his light gray slacks, some classic black and white Adidas sneakers and the white v-neck tee he wore. Amber masked it quickly, but I could see a gleam come and go in her eyes as she circled behind him. I knew she had a thing for him, but so far he'd rebuffed her advances, claiming she was too young for him and "Guards don't date Guards."

Moving on to me, she seemed to approve of my all-black jeans, Frye combat boots and t-shirt. I'd tried to tame my crazy hair, but Amber just reached up and messed it up again, grinning like the annoying sprite that she was. I caught Siri narrow her eyes at the contact, and grinned back. The girls agreed we'd do and we headed out the door for Zora's, where Amber's favorite DJ was spinning that night.

Inside the huge commercial building with blacked out windows and soundproofed walls, we waited in a hallway to go through the bouncer, Amber bopping around to the booming Tribal bass coming through the inner doors.

"Is this place a private club or something?" Siri asked me.

"Zora? Nah. Anyone can come here, although it is a something of a favorite for all the local Light fae, more than any other club. The owners are fae, and most of the employees, too. There are quite a few of us in Montreal, since it's so close to an Aeden portal."

Amber's long pigtails bounced as she bumped and wiggled to the music.

"Hey Amber, what's up? Tribe is spinning something fierce tonight. Ewan, Alec. Go on in." He nodded and waved our group in, where Native American pow-wow singing blended with a strong bass and fast beats.

"I'll get the first round," Ewan yelled over the music. Amber grabbed Siri's hand and dragged her away, pushing her way through the crowd of dancers, and I went to grab seats where I could keep an eye on the girls.

For almost an hour Ewan and I knocked back beers, watching them. Both of us quiet, thinking our own thoughts. Both of us grim. I knew my friend well enough to see that despite his resistance, he felt something for Amber, and tonight, he looked a little more bleak. A little more defeated.

I felt for him, but right now, I had my own demons to fight. I watched Siri move, at one with the music, graceful and catlike. Her aura flamed out in all directions, overwhelming the dim lights of the humans, even the brighter glows of the fae. She was like a lighthouse in a storm. Bright. Inexorable. Pulling me in. I was about to look away, when all of sudden her aura flickered and turned to mud. The color of fear. She'd stopped dancing and was staring into the crowd. Without hesitation, I moved to her, putting my hands on her arms and turning her to face me. She felt unnaturally cold, so I pulled her into my arms while I scanned the room for danger. Almost instantly, the heat of the surge started to thrum through me, warming me, and probably her, too. Her aura brightened as she leaned her head against me.

A moment later, cutting through my scan of the crowd, her voice made me look down into bright silver eyes. They were slightly out of focus, and I wondered if she'd had another vision.

"What detergent do you guys use?" she asked. Okay. She'd managed to surprise me again.

"Um. Some generic brand, I think. I don't know, Amber does all the laundry. Are you okay? You looked…"

"Yeah, I'm fine." She gazed up at me, starting to sway as a slow trance tune filled the room. I wasn't ready to let go of her, so I had no choice but to move with her. My hands roamed down her back on their own, landing on her hips, pulling her against me roughly. I wasn't touching her skin now, and I should have been relieved but instead I felt frustrated. Aching. A growl rose from my chest and I brushed my thumbs up under her camisole, gently rubbing the smooth skin above her belt. I'd never felt like this, not with any woman I'd ever been with. I could see her aura lighting up, practically filling the dance floor, and mine grew with it, intertwining so that the colors swirled together like a silvery pink and teal sun that threatened to explode through me at any moment. She leaned into me again, resting against my chest and we breathed as one.

"What is this?" she moaned.

My breath hitched. She didn't even know what the surge was. More than anything else, through the surge I had been able to feel not just her pleasure and wonder, but her full acceptance of it. Of me. She didn't know anything about the fae world, from what I had gathered. Somehow, Fred had managed to keep her completely innocent of all things fae. She didn't know what was happening, but I did. I knew better, at least, I thought I did. Christ, she had a boyfriend. I had to stop this. Now. My body shook with the effort of it, but I set her away from me. The loss of contact was painful, bring every drop of loneliness I'd ever felt crashing back down on top of me.

I gritted my teeth. "I need a drink. Come on."

I walked to the bar where Amber had her arm around Ewan and was giggling. Ewan slid a beer over to me and I stared down into its depths, looking for a way out of this sudden hellhole. Siri avoided me, squeezing between Amber and some guy who'd been trying to hit on her.

"Hey, girl," Amber exclaimed. "Here, we've been saving these for you." She pushed two amber shots towards Siri, and a tall glass of water. Siri eyed the shots warily. Right, I thought. American. She probably never drank.

"I don't know if our caretakin' duties extend to gettin' the faeling drunk, luv," Ewan admonished.

Amber protested, and Siri looked determined, picking up the first shot.

"Well, I think I deserve a little fun."

She downed both shots, one after the other, then coughed. I tried not laugh, really, but she was adorable as hell. Unfortunately, she caught me doing it, made a face and waved the bartender back over.

"Another round for all of us." She held up the shot glass, and gestured to the four of us. The guy nodded and grabbed a bottle of high-end Tequila, pouring out four more shots.

"Siri, I don't think—" I started. She threatened me with a look and grabbed one of the tiny glasses.

"Cheers!" she said, smiling sweetly at me with a wink, and downed the shot. I tried hard to look disapproving, but couldn't help a twinge of admiration that she managed not to cough this time.

The DJ announced the start of his second set and Amber pulled Siri back onto the dance floor. Siri danced like a demon possessed this time around. I tensed when a circle of guys crowded around them, getting handsy, but relaxed when I saw Siri was able to manage them herself. Still, watching her hips move to the music was setting me on edge. I looked away, determined not to enjoy the view.

"What the hell does she think she's playing at?" Ewan muttered, slamming down his beer. I looked up, expecting Siri to be causing some trouble, but she was dancing alone, as before. Then I saw Amber, staring defiantly at Ewan while she allowed one of her admirers to run his hands over her waist as she leaned back against him, dancing suggestively. Ewan crossed his arms, glaring back at her.

"You can't have it both ways, man," I laughed, shaking my head and taking another sip of my beer.

He grunted and narrowed his eyes, never taking them off her. Finally, with a sigh, he marched over, pulling her away from the guy she'd been dancing with.

The guy protested and Ewan ignored him, focusing only on Amber. I couldn't hear what he said to her, but I saw Amber smile and batt her eyelashes up at him. Well played, I thought.

Suddenly he reached down, threw her over his shoulder, and stalked off toward the exit.

"See you later, Siri!" Amber called, her laughter echoed through the club while people watched, bemused. Ewan didn't know it, but the staff here had set up a pool months ago on when he would finally cave. I'd just lost $100 bucks, but it was totally worth it.

Siri got back to dancing, finding a group of girls to join. Every once in a while a guy would try to approach her, but after a few glares from me they would give up. Soon enough, everyone left her alone to enjoy the music, while I switched to nursing a glass of water and trying to keep an eye on her without actually *watching* her.

She danced for hours, never tiring, never stopping, even though sweat glistened on her skin. The girls around her left, last call came and went, and still she danced. Any minute, the DJ would end his set, so I went out to the coat check to grab our things.

When I returned, she was sitting at the bar drinking some water. I draped her jacket over her shoulder unable to resist brushing my hand along her shoulder.

"Ready?" I asked.

She nodded, finishing her water.

We walked in silence back to the house. I thought about saying something, acknowledging this thing between us, the surge, but I couldn't. What was I supposed to say? No. Better to let her get to Valhalla, meet Bran, first. Let her figure out things with her boyfriend. Give her a chance to see what being fae was really about. And the doors her father could open for her. And maybe this yearning I was feeling would fade.

Back at the safehouse, she stalked off to my room, leaving me alone. I kicked off my boots and collapsed onto one of the couches, staring up at the ceiling. With my earth powers, the ambient light of the city night lit up the room more than I would have liked. It didn't matter. Somehow, I knew I wasn't going to get much rest. I stared at the ceiling, thinking. The clock on the stove read 3:48 am. I grabbed a pillow and jammed it under my head, pulled a throw blanket over my eyes, and hoped for sleep to come.

Silver eyes teased me, beckoned me to follow, into the dark. Giving up all resistance, I did, sinking into the blackness of dreams, chasing that platinum shine all the way.

CHAPTER 7

The next morning, Mitch Slaight stormed through the front door of the apartment, slamming it shut with a vengeance.

"Well, good morning to you, too," I said, propping my head up under one arm. Mitch was pissed about something, and I had a pretty good idea what it might be.

"Are you kidding me? Do you know how many texts I got this morning from Zora while I was waiting in line at the coffee shop, complaining about all the money he lost?"

Zora was the owner of the club we'd been at, and a pretty good friend of Mitch's. No one had expected Ewan to cave to Amber's demands so soon, least of all Zora. We shouldn't have underestimated the sprite's willpower.

"He's not the only one," I laughed.

"You think this is funny? Why didn't you tell me people were betting on Ewan getting it on with my damn niece? I didn't even know anything was going on between them. Some warning would have been nice, Ward."

I shrugged. "It wasn't really any of my business."

"Did you have a bet going, too?"

I coughed. "Well-"

"Right. I thought so. And now I am going to have to contact her parents, and explain what has happened to their baby girl on my watch." He groaned, putting his head in his hands. "I am never, ever going to hear the end of this."

Right on cue, Amber and Ewan came out of his room, holding and nuzzling each other as they walked, like some cheesy scene out of a chick flick.

"Hello there, Light Guards," Mitch said in his best captain's voice.

Ewan looked up and went pale. Amber rolled her eyes and went straight to espresso machine, setting it up to make enough for everyone.

"Looks like we're gonna need reinforcements," she muttered. "Did you at least bring breakfast?"

"Breakfast?" Mitch narrowed his eyes at his niece. "No, sorry, I was too busy fielding calls from all the people who lost the pool at Zora's to worry about feeding you. Why, work up an appetite, did you?"

"Actually," she said, winking at Ewan, "yeah, we did."

I laughed and Ewan collapsed on the couch next to me, burying his head.

"Please tell me she didn't," he groaned.

"Yeah," I managed to wheeze out between laughs. "She did."

"That's it young lady. I want you to pack your bags, 'cause you're going back to Aeden today. Whatever this is?" He gestured wildly between Amber and Ewan. "It's not happening, not now, not on my watch."

All the noise must have woken Siri up, because she came trudging out into the living room just then, wearing the same shirt from the night before and a pair of old grey sweats. Her hair was a wild nest of golden honey. Even as one hand tried to straighten it out, I wanted to mess it up again.

"Hey, what's all the racket?" she asked.

"You don't get to tell me what to do, not on this," Amber shouted at Mitch, standing toe to toe with him.

"Look, Amber, your parents trust me to keep you safe. When you signed up to be a Guardian, I promised them I would do my best to keep you out of trouble."

I laughed again, "Well, there was your first mistake."

They didn't even bother to look at me as they both said, "Shut up."

"Look Mitch, who I have a relationship with is none of your damned business. They want me alive, not celibate."

Ewan groaned, sinking his head even further into his hands.

"Oh, it's a relationship now, is it?" Mitch snorted.

Siri came and sat on the floor next to me. "What happened?" she whispered.

I brought her up to speed while she watched them continue to argue. Me? I watched her.

Finally, Ewan must have said something that won both Amber and Mitch over, because Amber squealed and jumped on his lap, throwing her arms around him.

Mitch sighed. "It's your funeral. I'll put in a good word for you with her father, see if we can't keep you alive for the rest of the relationship," he smirked. His eyes drifted over to me on the sofa, and he seemed to notice Siri for the first time.

"Well, hello there. Sorry if we woke you. As you can see, we had a little bit of family drama to sort out this morning." He walked over holding out his hand and she jumped up to shake his hand.

"It's nice to meet you, sir. I'm Siri Alvarsson."

"Yes, I know. You look very much like your mother. She was a student of mine years ago. Wonderful girl."

He smiled warmly at her.

"What about you, Alec, why are you on the couch, couldn't you make it to your room last night? Just how drunk were you all?"

"No, sir," I got up and started folding the blanket. "Siri slept in my room. I only had a couple drinks last night, in case any situations arose." More like several, but Mitch didn't need to know that.

Mitch looked at Amber nuzzling Ewan's neck, and shut his eyes tightly as if in pain. "Well, it seems a situation did arise, unfortunately."

Siri covered a laugh and I had to fight to keep in my own amusement.

"Yes, sir, sorry about that, sir. I felt it prudent to focus my attention on Siri."

"Yes. Well. About that. We think we have found where they are hiding Frederika, we have some operatives getting in position now. Ewan, you're going to stay here with me and wait so we can escort the team back to Aeden, assuming all goes well. Amber, you are going to ride back with Alec and Siri."

"Yeah, like I didn't see that coming from a mile away," she muttered. "Just can't wait to split us up, can you, Uncle?"

Mitch shook his head. "Look, you are still a Guard. Your new relationship is going to have to take a backseat to getting Siri safely back to Bran in Valhalla. The Shades have got to know we are closing in, and they're going to be getting desperate. We can't risk losing her when she's so close to safety."

"Fine," Amber looked at Siri. "You're right, sorry. I wasn't thinking. Can't have my new best bud getting snatched by the Dark, now can I? Besides, I think we have some catching up to do." She winked at her.

I groaned and decided it was good time to escape to take a shower.

"Not that I deserve to be stuck with two gossiping faelings," I said to myself.

"Hey now, I heard that," Amber yelled after me. "I'm not a faeling!"

I smiled, stripping down to my boxers when I got to my room and grabbing a clean pair of jeans from the closet. The door opened behind me, and I turned to see Siri staring at me with wide eyes.

I swallowed, and her eyes darkened as they traveled slowly down my torso. If I didn't get out of here quickly, Mitch would be giving a second sermon this morning.

"Sorry," I said loudly, "I'll get out of your way." I grabbed a shirt and some socks, brushing by her accidentally in my hurry to get out. Not quickly enough. Or maybe not slowly enough. In that instant, I felt the surge again, more powerfully than ever before, even if it was just for a moment.

I showered quickly, lathering up with the Irish Spring soap that was always on hand, thanks to Ewan, then got dressed and went back out to help myself to some coffee. I made small talk with Mitch, trying to keep his focus off Ewan. Finally, Amber bounced back into the room, dressed like more of a Japanese school girl than a Light Guard in striped pink and black leggings tucked into Doc boots, a Hello Kitty sweater and two perky buns on top of her head. Soon after, Siri came in, freshly showered, and we all said our goodbyes.

Amber and I climbed in the front of Ewan's '66 Scout while Siri and Miko sprawled across the backseat. We'd hardly been on the road for two minutes before her stomach growled loudly.

"Dude, was that you?" Amber asked her.

"I guess so," she said. "I haven't eaten anything since last night's poutine, what about you guys?"

"Nah, me neither," Amber replied. "My uncle kind of found us before Ewan and I had a chance to put anything together."

"Oh, I don't know, I think you guys had plenty of luck putting things together, if you know what I mean." I leered at her.

"Ew! You are such a skag." She swatted me. "Alright, change of plans, let's take Siri over to Chez Boris for some breakfast beignets and cocoa. You are going to love this place, they have the best doughnuts in all of Montreal; they even make doughnut sandwiches."

"I like the way you think, Amber," I said, turning the car around.

Inside the quaint, sugary smelling café, Siri seemed to want to stay to eat, but I vetoed the idea, insisting on hitting the road. The sooner I passed her off to Bran, the better. Amber picked out twelve donuts, several breakfast 'beignewiches' and three extra-large hot chocolates.

Outside, Siri grabbed a donut, moaning as she walked and ate. I stalked ahead, not able to take her sounds of pleasure. Was she torturing me on purpose? No. I knew the donuts were just that good. But come on. Give a guy a break.

Behind me, she yelled, sounding pissed, and I spun around to see her pulling forward into a crouch, flipping a large man over her shoulder onto his back. She stared down at him, frozen momentarily, and he used the time to grab her by the neck, pulling her head down. As I rushed forward, she snapped her shoulder forward, jabbing her elbow into the Shade's face. His head fell back just as Amber leaped over her head aiming a flying kick at another Dark fae to knock him out.

Problems solved.

I reached down to help her stand. "We've got to get out of here, others might be on the way already. Not to mention, we have a bit of an audience," I said, watching some young girls across the street filming us.

"Oh, fans!" Amber gave them a wide smile and a dainty bow before she linked arms with Siri. "Don't worry, our IT guys will have scrubbed the video from the internet by lunchtime."

Back on the road, I ate and drove as fast as traffic would allow. For all Amber's optimism, I knew that the incident with the two thugs wasn't a coincidence. The Morrigan was looking for us, and we needed to get out of Midgard as soon as possible, down to the safety of Aeden. Amber slept in the back seat now, and Siri sat beside me, eating and staying quiet as she watched the trees pass by on the highway.

I didn't bother trying to make conversation. What was there to say?

Soon enough, she'd have a whole new life. Mine wouldn't change. I'd keep chasing Shades, and protecting

Aeden. Shielding the light fae, making sure the innocent stayed that way.

CHAPTER 8

Driving for hours, and I still couldn't stop replaying the attack in my mind. A few times, I kicked the adrenaline, only to have it creep back in. The idea of what could have happened to her if the Shades had succeeded... Twinges of guilt and fear nagged at me, reminding me of the past. I hadn't let anyone get under my skin like this is years, not since I'd found out that not everyone in Aeden was considered equal.

When I'd first arrived, ten years old, still reeling from the shock of finding my family literally in pieces, my father had dumped me with a family he knew and left with barely a word. That day had changed both of us, him more than me. If I was in shock, he was shattered and re-forged in cold hard steel. My father's name was Flynn, but over the years I came to nickname him "Flint" in my head. Not that I would have dared call him that out loud. The love and the smiles he'd had for me as a child disappeared that day, when he became dedicated to the task of finding my mother and sister's killers. Even after he had his vengeance, he didn't soften. The father I knew died that day with my mother.

But kids bounce, you know? So when I started school, I made new friends pretty quickly. Not with everyone. Some people looked down on me because of my Midgard origins. Like every school, ours had its bullies and I tried not to pay them much mind, unless they were bugging someone who couldn't defend themselves. Which was actually how I made a few of my friends, sticking up for them when no one else would.

One new friend had a grandmother who doted on me when she visited for a few months, baking me cookies and treating me like her own child. Whatever was broken inside me, her gentle smiles and comforting after-school teas helped heal it.

Still, I could never forget what I had seen.

So, when it came time for my friends and I to choose the tracks in school that would determine our future occupations, Light Guard was the obvious choice. It meant I wouldn't see my friends as often, because most of them were going into more peaceful tracks like The Sciences or Realm Histories. But I assumed we would still see each other after school. That we would still have each other's backs.

I was wrong.

When it came down to it, my old friends decided being a simple Light Guard was beneath them. Same for being friends with one. That stung. Left with nothing, again, I'd thrown myself into my studies, vowing to perfect every move, every tactic the teachers could throw at me. Instead of tea with nice old fae-mothers, I spent every evening training, studying, learning. Until I was the best in my year. Until I was tossing my instructors on their backs. Until I knew I would be able to save anyone, anywhere, any time. No one would ever be hurt again, not on my watch.

In a way, I had become as single-minded as my father.

And today, I'd almost blown it. The Dark had touched her, while I'd been mere feet away. My failure ate at me.

"I'm sorry for what happened back there." I had to say it. Had to try and get rid of this feeling, this weight.

"It's not like it was your fault," Siri said.

I checked the rearview mirror before I answered, gripping the wheel. Amber snored gently in the back seat with Miko draped around her neck.

"No, but I should have been paying more attention. Mitch warned us there might be danger. And I should never have let you walk by yourself behind us like that."

"Hey now, I think I took care of myself pretty well back there. I might not know all your fancy moves, but I was trained by the best, you know." She was trying to tease me, to laugh it off, but I couldn't do that.

"Yeah, but not the best of the best," I said, thinking of the limits of her training. Frederika was good, amazing even, but she had never studied glima or lasair. "We will remedy that in Valhalla. I have a feeling you are going to need that training before too long. Besides," I smiled, trying not to sound too uptight, "how else will you be able to hold your own in a spar with me?"

"Oh, I can think of some ways, don't worry." She grinned. The fact that she thought that drove home just how badly she needed more training, wiping the smile off my face.

"Those guys, we were lucky, they don't seem to have been well-trained," I said.

"I saw them looking at their phone when we came out from the doughnut shop, I think maybe they were looking at a picture of me. Is that possible?"

"Yeah, the Dark is probably broadcasting your face to every Shade that has a phone, probably with some kind of reward. Like I said, we were lucky." I didn't like it. Didn't like relying on luck, rather than skill. Luck could get you killed.

"Well, I'd like to think skill had at least a little bit to do with it."

"No." I shook my head in frustration. "You don't understand. As good as the Light Guardians are, the Shades have trained fighters who are just as good. Some of them are so twisted and evil, it is almost impossible to fight them. Some of them feel no pain, and are fueled by pure bloodlust. They revel in it."

Fingers, lined up neatly on the coffee table. Blood on the walls. Hair on the floor. The memories crowded me, eclipsing the road.

Then, like the sun on a cloudy day, warmth and comfort flowed through my arm, from her hand to me. I could feel her compassion. Her caring. She had such a big, open heart. Mine felt shriveled in comparison to what I felt pumping through her. I'd never felt that potential, that capacity for caring, from anyone.

"You sound like you're talking from personal experience," she said. "I'm sorry if taking care of me is bringing up some bad memories."

"Thanks," I smiled at her, glancing at her arm. I could actually see flashes of light flowing between us, traveling into me. Quickly, I looked back at the road. I relaxed into the feeling and tried to keep my mind on driving at the same time. Have you ever had to do anything like that?

It's not easy.

I couldn't form a single thought, and had to fight the urge to pull over and take her in my arms. Claim her for mine. Whether I deserved her or not.

I was just about to do it, too, when she pulled her hand away, shuttering the sun back behind the clouds. Rational thought came back and I remembered what we'd been talking about. She deserved to know. To understand why I took my job so seriously. Why I was the way I was. What should I say?

I decided to start at the beginning

"It happened when I was just a boy. My father fell in love with a human, my mother. He left Aeden and fae politics behind him to make her happy. Before, he'd been with the Guardians, but we lived in Boston for most of my childhood. He trained me from an early age, a lot like how your mom trained you. My sister hated fighting, all she ever wanted to do was dance, and he let her. She was three years younger than me."

70

I stopped, remembering Farrah's sweet little voice, the way she would just spin and spin in the kitchen for hours.

"One day, the Dark sent men to our house to capture my dad. He may have put fae matters aside, but his name was still in their records as an operative, and they'd found him. We were out fishing. It was a gorgeous day, a lot like this one. I'd caught five trout all by myself, and I felt so proud coming home to show my mom. But when we got there, my mother and sister were dead. They'd been tortured, beaten and killed without remorse. The house was covered in blood. We didn't even get to bury them, my father packed me back in the car immediately and took me to Aeden to live. I was only ten, but I dedicated my life to becoming a Guardian that day."

"Oh Alec, I'm so sorry. All this time, I never thought anyone could understand how I am feeling about my mom, but this has got to be so difficult for you, bringing it all back."

I shrugged. I was used to the memories. She didn't understand what was really tearing me apart.

"The Dark stopped scaring me a long time ago. I didn't think they could ever hurt me again. But the thought of them getting to you...I won't let that happen."

"Is that the surge talking, or some Guardian kind of honor code?" She clapped a hand over her mouth, like she hadn't meant to say that. I tried to think what to say. Part of me wanted to pull over again, knowing that she felt what I was feeling. The other part of me wanted to strangle Ewan, Amber and Mitch for having introduced her to the idea of the surge, for giving her a name for the feelings. Knowing what it was would make it harder to resist, and I had every intention of resisting.

"I don't know," I answered carefully, avoiding eye contact. I decided to downplay the whole situation. "I want to protect you. Discovering you with a darkling made me want to rip your friend's head off, and not just because I hate the Dark. But your father is Bran, so I think...I think you must be meant for something big, given who your family is, and the way Mikael is hunting for you. I'm not sure we could ever-"

A loud yawn from the backseat interrupted me. "Whatcha guys talking about? Is he schooling you on the ways of the Dark?" Amber rubbed her eyes and leaned over the seat. Thank Odin she'd stopped me before I could say something stupid. "What'd I miss?"

"Nothing," Siri and I answered at the same time.

We made small talk and drove a few more miles, finally arriving in front of a tiny, ancient wood cabin in the deep woods.

"Don't worry, the cabin's just for show," Amber whispered to Siri. "We almost never stay in it."

"Speak for yourself, girly girl," I said. "I love staying out here. It's really quiet, if you know what I mean."

"Oh I totally get you," she rolled her eyes, "I love the quiet when you stay out here, too."

I ignored their giggles while I parked the Scout behind the cabin between some large bushes. Everyone got out and I took Siri's pack, putting it over my shoulder. The squirrel scampered away, taking to the trees while we walked into the woods. This time, Amber took lead and I brought up the rear. No one would get the jump on Siri ever again, not if I could help it.

Then Siri stumbled and stopped, the squirrel chattering loudly enough to wake the dead above us. I crashed into her while she hissed Amber's name, trying to call her back.

"What is it?" I whispered in her ear, on alert. She shivered in my arms and I gripped her shoulders.

"Shades, five of them, up ahead."

"How do you-"

"Miko," she gestured with her chin.

"Okay." I said. This squirrel was really beginning to grow on me. If nothing else, he made a great sentinel. "Stay out of the clearing. I'm going to go around and close the circle from behind. Whatever you do, don't follow Amber. She can take care of herself."

"Whatever you say, oh Captain my Captain."

I ignored the Dead Poet's line and hoped she'd stay put, while I left her behind and crept further into the forest. I knew these woods well, and took a small deer path around to the north so I could come up on the Shades from behind. It meant I would lose some time, but the element of surprise would more than make up for it. With just five Shades, I knew Amber could handle herself until I got there. Knowing her, she was probably dazzling them with her "little lost girl" routine. People always underestimated Amber because of her club girl style and small stature. Those people usually came to regret it.

Muffled voices carried through the trees. Amber laughing. Probably twirling her hair. Stringing them along. Just another minute and I would be in position.

The voices rose, and the unmistakable sounds of fighting. I swore. They'd started without me.

I picked up the pace and flew towards the clearing. I wasn't where I was hoping to be, but it would have to do.

I pulled out my throwing knives as I ran, three for each hand, and dashed up a series of rocks to perch on a boulder near the opening of the cave.

All the breathe left my lungs as I saw Amber and Siri standing back to back, Siri frozen in place while a small wiry man with a predatory gaze held her neck in his hands. Breathe Alec, I told myself. But she didn't move. Didn't try to evasive maneuvers. And I knew something had to be wrong if she wasn't fighting back. My angle was all wrong and it was a risky shot, but I didn't think twice. While Amber was preoccupied fending off a long haired First Nations guy with tribal tattoos and a wild looking redheaded woman, we were already losing the fight.

The first 5-inch dagger flew without thought, straight into the eye of the rat holding Siri. His hands opened and he dropped without a sound. Siri whipped around, seeing me, and I breathed for the first time since entering the clearing.

No time, the other shades had seen their companion go down, and before they could react I was leaping off the boulder, running at them, aiming flying daggers into their spines and kidneys. Amber's would-be attackers crumpled to the ground before they had a chance to assess the new threat.

Me.

"Nice work, Bruce Lee. I was wondering when you'd show up," Amber quipped, but I barely heard her. Blood roared in my head, making it impossible to think of anything.

Except her.

She'd almost died.

Would it have killed her to listen to me? To stay put? To let me do my job? How could I protect someone who was a constant danger to herself?

Was she hurt?

Somehow, I found myself standing in front of Siri, drawn in like an imperial cruiser to the Death Star. My hand made its way to her cheek, cradling it gently while I fired questions at her in random order.

"What the hell happened back there? You stopped fighting. Why? And why were you fighting in the first place? What about 'stay here' did you not understand?"

I was so relieved she wasn't hurt, and so angry she'd put herself in danger that part of me wanted to teach her a lesson myself.

How could she? How could she put herself in danger like that?

Didn't she know that I-?

She reached up and placed two fingers over my lips, contact both too little and too much.

"Shh. It's okay." She removed her fingers. "I'm okay."

"But you-"

Under my hand, I could feel her cheek burning like fire, burning through me. I could feel the surge pulling me to her, wanting to draw all that fire into me.

I couldn't do it.

But she could.

She reached up around the back of my head and drew me down to kiss her, rising up to meet me like a wave breaching the shore.

Her desire slammed into me, I could feel it, the heat and the passion she contained within her, and I don't just mean her lips. No, I could *feel* what she was feeling, the emotions whirling through her heart, surging and threatening to overtake us both.

For a second, I felt her doubt herself, felt her begin to pull back, but I wasn't about to let go. Not now, not when I had just begun to discover what this was. I knew the surge was supposed to be powerful. But Amber and Ewan were the only people I knew personally who'd experienced it, and they had never described just what it felt like. I hadn't know that when you connected, it was like you shared one heart, like you could *feel* and know everything the other person was feeling.

Her heart was so much bigger than mine. Mine had broken apart years ago, and no one had ever really bothered to help me put it back together. Hers... It felt as big as the sun itself, and as intense. She pretended she was tough. But inside, she was pure love. Pure light. I hadn't known such people existed.

Just feeling it, made me want to know more, feel more. To climb inside of it and live within its warm glow forever. If my heart had been shattered when I was ten, I could feel the heat of her light melting the jagged edges, preparing it to be fused back together. Just a little more, a little longer.

It wouldn't take long. Just forever.

The sound of Amber clapping brought me back to my senses.

We pulled apart, and I stared at her, entranced, watching the glow of her aura shimmering around her so that she was encased in its rosy hue.

"That was. Amazing," she murmured, breathing heavily.

"Woo hoo, Alec and the commander's daughter, this is going to be awesome!" Amber laughed.

She might as well have doused me with a bucket of ice water. What had I done? Nothing had changed.

I took a step back.

I didn't know how I would go back. How I could go back, to what I was before.

But nothing had changed. She wasn't for me. I knew that, as surely as I knew that I would never find another woman like her, another heart to set fire mine.

"I'm sorry, I shouldn't have...I mean, we can't-" I stammered, the words coming out with no clear direction or ending.

"Hey, whatever, you didn't do anything. Forget it." Her face turned into a stony mask and she leaned down to grab the bloody knife from the rat's eye, wiping it on the ground and sticking it in her boot. "If you don't mind, I'll keep this until you can deliver me to my father."

"Siri, look, let's talk." Even without touching her, I knew she was thinking of using it on me, next. I couldn't see a way for us, but whatever I'd said had come out wrong. So wrong. The proof was in her eyes.

"Hey, there's nothing to talk about. You're just doing your job, and I have a darkling boyfriend, remember?" she said, as if I needed reminding. Her words hurt, but not as much as she had intended. The warmth of the surge still hadn't faded, not entirely, not for me. Maybe she was the one who'd needed reminding, not me. I smiled as I watched her stalk away with Amber and Miko in tow.

I gave her the space she needed, collecting the rest of my knives before I followed, humming quietly under my breath.

Humming, and smiling.

Smiling, and thinking.

CHAPTER 9

When I reached the golden gravicycles lined up in the main cavern, the girls were laughing and already seated tandem on one of the flying machines.

Perhaps I shouldn't have given them so much space, I thought, remembering the feel of Siri against my back on the Ducati.

I brushed away the thought, turning my mind to the trip back to Valhalla. Soon, I would be back in the Light Guard Command Center, and I needed to get my head together.

They set off, steadily picking up speed down another dark tunnel. The dim UV headlights of the gravicycle lit up the naturally fluorescing rocks on the walls in vivid greens, whites and purples. Always a demon on a gravicycle, Amber's speed continued to increase. The rocks in the tunnel streamed by in a blur, shimmering brilliantly under my enhanced vision. Once, I saw Siri turn, looking for me in the dim light, but I knew she couldn't see me behind the glare of the bike's headlights.

Finally, the light of the Aeden sky appeared at the end of the tunnel. Amber gunned her motor, and so did I, increasing my speed to burst out into the light. For a moment, the red glare of Anansanna, the warm Aeden sun, was blinding. And then, my eyes adjusted and I grinned, happy.

Home again.

Pink and peach clouds dotted the sky, the remnants of a storm that had recently passed. The air was hot and humid, with an incredibly clean ozone tang to it. Aeden air. My lungs filled with the pure sweetness of it and I grinned as I went even faster, zooming past the girls to feel the rush of wind in my hair.

It wasn't enough. I needed more. Something to take my mind off the girl behind me. Something else to make my blood pulse. I flipped the auto-pilot on and climbed up to stand on the seat of the cycle, and threw my head back in a wild yell.

Better.

I spread my arms, closed my eyes and breathed deeply.

Much better.

I hopped back down on my seat, smiling.

The rest of the long ride was smooth, easy. When the golden spires of Valhalla rose into view they brought me back to reality. The Tree of Life at their center, so huge and tall, taunted me, making me think of Vala's words about fate and trust.

Below, Tower Three beckoned and we obeyed, slowly descending onto the gravicycle deck like leaves upon the breeze.

"Welcome to Valhalla!" Mireia Yamuun, the chief emissary of Valhalla greeted us. Tall and gorgeous as ever, she walked across the balcony and bowed before Siri with her mahogany hands steepled in the universal prayer pose of respect.

"You must be Siri. I am Mireia. Your father was hoping to be here to welcome you, but he has been called into council to deal with another matter. Please, why don't you come with me and I can show you to your room so you can freshen up. I am sure by the time you are finished he will be available to see you all." She smiled at us all, and led the way inside the tower. Amber and I removed our shoes before entering, mindful of the life-giving cala grass that carpeted the halls indoors, and I watched Siri do the same.

I enjoyed the cool boost of energy that flowed instantly through the soles of my feet when I stepped on the cala, and saw Siri pause and wiggle her toes in the blue plants.

"What kind of carpet is this?" she asked.

"Carpet? I'm sorry, I'm not familiar with that word," Mireia replied.

"We don't use carpets in Aeden, we use cala," I said. "What you are walking on right now is actually a hybrid cross between the plant you call grass and a thick ground clover. It's pretty hardy, but walking shoeless helps it stay healthy. We all have a deep connection to the plant life in Aeden. Can you feel how it nourishes you? Right now, your immune system is actually regenerating your cells at a faster speed because of the biosynthesis going on between you and the cala."

"Wow, cool."

We waited for her to move on, and then walked her to her room. They'd assigned her the Norna visiting suite, its door marked with a triskele. The symbol represented the family's seer heritage, linking past, present and future. I'd escorted Bran's mother here several times when she was visiting. It was much larger than my own Guard accomodations, which were a simple single room with bed, dresser, a desk, some chairs and a bathroom.

Mireia and Siri put their hands over the triskele, keying the door so it would now open only for Siri, and her assigned companion. Siri seemed surprised that she was being given the equivalent of a ladies maid and I smirked. She had no idea how important she really was, who her father was. Just another difference between her circumstances and my own.

Mireia helped settle her in, while the young maid excused herself to run a bath for Siri. Amber hugged Siri, and Mireia told her she'd be back in an hour to take her to meet her father. To meet Bran. I should have left right then. Bran was waiting for me, I knew. Waiting to debrief me. But I stood, frozen. This was it. Everything was changing now, I could feel it. I stared at the bowl of pink and white fruits on the table while the others left.

I should say something. I knew I should. But what?

"So, a red sun and purple trees, huh?" Siri waved at the scene outside the window, awkwardly breaking the silence between us. "You know, you guys could have warned me about some of this."

"Would you have believed me?" I asked in a low voice.

"Hmm, let's see. We just came fifty miles through the earth's mantle, and we're in a giant gold castle watching the sun set from inside the earth? Um, no, I guess not." She laughed.

"Actually, the sun never sets here in Aeden, and it was more like two hundred miles." I smiled back at her, some of the awkwardness dissipating. "It's part of why the fae here live longer. The lack of ways to mark the passage of our days affects how our minds, and thus our bodies, view time. It is a perfect power source, too, and it's also why you won't see many windows on the buildings that can't be completely sealed from the light."

"So, now what? Are you going to stick around, like Amber? Or are you going right back to the surface?" She tried to sound like she didn't care either way, but I knew what she was really asking. How could I not? I had the same questions.

"I'm not sure," I answered, nervously running a hand through my hair, guessing it was a mess after the gravicycle ride. "I have to debrief first with my commander."

"You mean my father?" she asked pointedly.

"Yeah, that, too." I sighed.

"Amber mentioned our families were really close. I guess that means we're practically cousins, right?" She laughed and sat down, striking a casual pose, the gleam in her eyes anything but. "Look, just so we're clear, I didn't mean to cause you any trouble back there, you know, above below or whatever. I know you were just doing your job. Okay?"

"Don't worry about it," I said, shoving my hands in my pockets. She'd said it herself. She had a boyfriend. And all I had to do was look around her room to see that we didn't belong together. But how could I tell her those things when everything inside was screaming at me to make her mine? "I handled that badly. I don't want you to think I took advantage of you. I really...well, look, like you said, you have a guy already. You've been attacked three times in as many days. I was supposed to be taking care of you, not-"

"Yeah, yeah, I get it." She jumped out of her seat and marched up to me. "I'm just a faeling you'd rather not be babysitting." Her voice rose, dripping with sarcasm. "I'm oh so sorry to have caused you all this trouble. At least you can go debrief now and get rid of all this drama, go back above below and save someone else now." She gave me a small shove, just enough to drive her point home.

Just enough to push me to take her.

"Look here, Siri," I warned, taking a step towards her. Suddenly, her face softened, and she looked up at me sadly. Like she *missed* me. Like I was the one rejecting her.

Against my better judgment, I took another step towards me. "Please, can't we just talk?"

"I-"

84

"Your bath, miss, it's ready for you." The attendant came in, a young slip of girl with white blonde hair, interrupting whatever Siri had been about to say. "You should probably go now, sir."

The young girl watched me like I was dangerous, and she wasn't wrong. I didn't belong here. I should just leave. Instead, without meaning to, I took another step forward and whispered in Siri's ear. Forbidden words, that the other girl could not hear.

"This isn't over. Think about what you want to say to me while I am gone. Because, as much as I would like otherwise, I will be thinking about you."

Then, before I could think of what I had said, what I had started, I turned and left.

CHAPTER 10

Amber was already in the room with Bran when I arrived, bringing him up to speed on the attacks in Montreal and at the camp. While she talked, I watched Bran's face light up with pride as she described the way Siri had fought each time. He hadn't even met her, and already he was playing the part of father.

Flynn hadn't looked at me like that in over a decade. No. Everything I did, everything I'd *become*, was exactly what he expected of me. Nothing more, not in his eyes. Anything more would have required some sort of filial connection, something that had died with the women in my family.

Looking at Bran's eyes, the truth was obvious. The same liquid silver gaze, wise and wry. Siri may have resembled her mother more, feature for feature, but she had her father's unmistakable eyes. Like Siri and Fred, too, he was known to be an earth fae.

Amber wrapped up her tale and Bran turned to me.

"Anything you would like to add, Ward?"

"Everything before Montreal went smoothly. I picked her up at Vala's, like you asked, and brought her to the safehouse. At Vala's we sparred a little outside, and she has significant training from Frederika, as Amber told you. She says she hasn't had her Choosing yet, but her earth powers are already manifesting."

"Mmm, yes. Vala told me about that. She has some interesting ideas about Siri's future." He gazed at me without expression, and I prayed that Vala hadn't said anything to him about Siri's forest visions of me. She might be a Druid advising the Commander, but some things should be kept private, right?

"Did she?" I asked, keeping my voice light.

"Yes." His face remained an unreadable mask.

"Well, like I said, her powers are already manifesting, so I assume they will be significant once they develop fully. What did Vala say?"

"Nothing that concerns you at the moment. Right now, what you need to worry about is getting above below and finding a lead on the cure for the anti-serum. I'm sending you to check out some medical research labs we believe operate on Shade funding. We have more people coming in every week stricken by this abomination, and Frederika is on her way in right now."

"They found her?" I asked.

"Yes. They used the anti-serum on her before we got to her, unfortunately, so your upcoming mission isn't just strategic now. It's personal. At least, for me." Bran looked weary, like he'd aged another five years since the last time I saw him. "I trust you will do your best."

"Always, sir." He didn't know it, but it was personal for me, too, now. I'd felt close to Frederika when she's trained me, and I'd do whatever they asked me to bring her back a cure. To give Siri back her mother.

Bran nodded, knowing my words were true.

"Now, Vala also mentioned that my daughter has befriended a darkling? She insists that he is no threat to my daughter, that he claims he wants to Choose the Light. Is this true?"

"Yes, sir." I thought for a moment. Remembered the magnitude of light I had felt when Siri kissed me. If Rowan had experienced even the smallest amount of the power in her heart when they connected, I imagined he would do whatever he could to stay with her. He'd have to be an idiot not to. And I'd seen the way he watched her when we were leaving. As much as it pained me to say it, I had to be honest. "I think he actually will. His parents have filled his head with all sorts of lies about the light, but Siri is...inspiring."

"Is she?" he mused. "Okay then. On your recommendation, I will heed Vala's counsel. She has asked us for help, when the time comes. His father is pure Dark, Odin knows he's caused us enough trouble in the past. I think you can guess what he will think of his son turning Light. Vala says she will host the boy's Choosing, but we must give him sanctuary here immediately after. When that happens, I think you should be his escort, since you've already met. It should soften the transition."

I looked at Amber and she quirked an eyebrow at me, daring me to say otherwise.

I ignored her. A mission was a mission. If this is what it took to keep Siri happy here in Valhalla, I would do it. I kept my face passive, while my heart beat like a drum.

"Of course. Is there anything else, sir?" Gods. What else could he ask of me? I'd never ignored an order. I wouldn't start now. If he asked me to cut out my heart, I would. Part of me felt like he already had.

"No, that's all for now. Get some rest, and head back to Montreal first thing in the morning. When you get there, Mitch will give you all the details of the mission."

"What about me, sir?" Amber asked.

"I want you to stick close to my daughter. You'll be her trainer, her guide and her guard. This is all new to her, and she's going to need a friend. From what you say, you've already made a connection, correct?"

"Yes, sir. We get along well. I'll make sure she settles in." The loose hairs that had escaped from her buns bobbed in agreement.

"See that you do," Bran stood, and walked to the windows, watching two hawks circle each other in the sky. "Dismissed."

Amber and I got up and left the room, walking past our fellow Light Guards at the door, Dorian and Barit. They ignored us, as we were all trained to do when on duty. Boring stuff, door duty, but everyone took their turn.

We got on the winding escalator and started spiraling down.

"So, you didn't tell Bran that his daughter is dating that darkling." Amber squinted at me, like she was examining some dirt on my face.

"Not my story to tell," I shrugged. "If Vala didn't think it was an important detail, why should I?"

"Hmm. I don't know. Maybe because you guys lip-locked in the woods? Or maybe because you're totally crazy about her?"

"What?" I crossed my arms and shook my head. "I don't know what you mean."

"Oh, please. You guys can't keep your eyes off each other. You're worse than me and Ewan."

I snorted. "No one's worse than you and Ewan."

She smiled, like she knew all my secrets. "Trust me. You guys? It's like, epic."

"Whatever." I shrugged and started walking down the stairs. Amber, of course, insisted on following.

"You do. You *like* her."

"Even if I did. What would it matter? She's the fricking Commander's daughter. You and I both know what that means."

She put a hand on my shoulder, stopping me, making me look at her. She was a couple steps up from me, so we were at eye level with each other. Her dark eyes stared deep into mine.

"It doesn't mean anything. You worry too much about stuff like that. You *like* her," she repeated.

I rolled my eyes and twitched my shoulder, shaking her off.

"I have to pack." I turned and walked away, down the escalator.

She stayed where she was, but her words followed me like a threat, or maybe a promise.

"Deny it all you want Alec, but you know it's true. You can't deny the surge!"

CHAPTER 11

Instead of packing, I went to the training arena, sparring with some fresh new Guards. Two hours of fighting took me to where I wanted to be. Bone tired and too sore to think. I grabbed a bite to eat from the Guards' mess hall and took my time getting back to my room.

There, it took me all of two minutes to pack and lay out the things I'd wear tomorrow. Remembering that Siri had one of my throwing knives, I pulled out a different set. These were my most lethal and prized knives, made from the black steel of Roumkivara. The blades were barbed, ensuring that they would do even more damage on the way out than they did on the way in. They were dangerous, and matched my mood perfectly.

I pulled off my rode-worn jeans and sweaty t-shirt, and ran a bath in my small tub. Easing into the steaming silvery Valhallan water, I closed my eyes and focused on the mind-clearing techniques I'd learned in training.

Breathing in, and breathing out.

Keeping thoughts far from my mind.

Keeping *her* far from my mind.

I sank into a deep state of tranquility, deep into the darkness of nothingness. Just where I wanted to be.

An insistent rapping at my outer door brought me out of it. The bath was icy, and my muscles had frozen up in the cold. I went under the water and came back up, shaking the water out of my hair.

Again, someone knocked. Louder this time.

"Yeah, yeah, just a minute!" I called.

I got out and wrapped a towel around my waist.

I gestured at the door, triggering the golden panel to slide into the wall.

"What?"

Amber barged in, pushing her way past me and almost dislodging my towel. Would have served her right. I scowled at her while she made herself at home in the chair next to my desk.

"Hey, Alec. All packed?"

"Yep." I waited for her to explain herself. Amber and I were friends, but we didn't usually visit each other in our rooms.

Instead of saying anything though, she just screwed up her face and started examining her nails, like she had all the time in the world.

"What do you want, Amber?"

"Me? Nothing." She looked up at me, wide eyes blinking innocently. The she gave me a sly smile. "This is about what you want."

I groaned.

"Amber, we already went over this," I started, like I was explaining things to a child. "I don't *want* anything."

"Liar."

"It's true, Amber. Now do you mind? I have an early start in the morning."

"Fine, fine. I'm going." She chuckled and started to head out the door.

"Great, I'll see you when I get back."

"Oh wait, I almost forgot!" She said dramatically, slapping a hand to her forehead and putting a hand on the doorway as she turned back. "I did have something to tell you. Something important. Though, maybe not, it's probably nothing."

"Spit it out, Amber," I ground out between my teeth. "Before I throttle you with this towel." I reached down to put a hand at my waist, seriously considering doing it, too.

"Okay, okay!" She laughed. "Geez. I just thought you might like to know...the darkling dumped Siri."

"What? Why?" Her words made no sense to me.

"From what I can gather, he let jealousy get the better of him."

"Jealousy? Because she's in Aeden?"

"No, you idiot. Because she's totally interested in someone else, and he could tell."

"What do you mean?"

"Gods, you're slow. You like her, she likes you, the darkling dumped her, now everybody's happy. Well, except the darkling. Whatever. I'm here, because I thought you should know before you leave. You know…before she meets some other handsome, dashing Guard and falls head over heels in surge with him."

"Amber, I told you-"

"I know, I know. You have absolutely 'no idea what I'm talking about'." She made air quotes with her fingers to emphasize the sarcasm. "Whatever. Just don't be an idiot too long, okay? I like this girl. She's perfect for you. Don't screw it up."

"Are you done?"

She grinned at me. "Peace out, give my man Ewan a big smooch for me, 'kay?"

And then she let go of the door and took a step back, letting the panel slide shut without a sound.

I didn't know what to think. I couldn't think. I reached into my dresser, grabbed the first pair of shorts I touched, and collapsed into bed. A flick of the bedside switches turned off the lights and plunged me into momentary darkness, until my eyes adjusted and I could see everything in perfect detail.

I closed my eyes and saw *her*.

I opened my eyes.

Dammit, Amber.

Everything had changed.

Nothing had changed.

Amber said that I cared too much about things that didn't matter, but I knew she was wrong. She'd never had to endure the taunts that I had, the teasing about my parents, the nicknames, the fights.

She was wrong.

Wasn't she?

My brain was on spin cycle, going around and around the problem for hours. Finally, well after midnight, I jumped off the bed and opened the bottom drawer in my desk.

It was a treasure trove of useful objects. Daggers. Journals. Cell phones and false passports.

But the one thing I wanted most, I couldn't find in the shadows. Frustrated, I strode to the window and released the sun shade, letting the outside light flood the room. The glare hurt my eyes, but I stood still for a moment, allowing my vision to adjust.

I took a deep breath, opened my eyes and walked back to the desk, yanking the drawer out and dumping the contents out on the bed.

Yes.

There.

I picked up the small golden card, embossed with the fine lines of Valhallan circuitry.

I'd made it back in my third year of Guard training, in Access class. Every Light Guard was expected to have at least a working knowledge of how to break through security alarms, pick locks, escape restraints, that sort of thing. For my final project, I'd paired up with a serious tech geek in the class, and we'd made a pair of all-access key cards that could open virtually any door in Valhalla. We'd gotten top marks, both of us, for our effort.

I'd never used it myself, only watched the professor open the Council's chambers with it.

Tonight, we'd see what doors it could open for me.

CHAPTER 12

The halls from my room to hers were quiet, and I passed no one on the way. No one that could have changed my mind. No one to deter me from my goal.

To see her, just see her one more time before I went.

The triskele on her door glinted in the bright hall lights, and I paused. One last chance to turn back. One last chance to let her go.

I couldn't do it.

Making sure I was alone in the hall first, I took the card out and held it against the doors, held my breath. Would it even work after all these years? A moment went by. Then two. The door slid open, and the only sound was me exhaling in relief.

I padded quietly into the room, walking past the couches and into the bedroom. The air was warm in the room, likely warmer than she was used to, and she'd kicked off her blankets. Like a goddess carved from amber, she lay on her back on the bed, sheathed in golden silk, her wheaten hair fanned around her head while she slept soundly.

Now more than ever, she truly looked the part of a princess.

Not knowing what I meant to do, not knowing where this could lead, I climbed up onto the bed and straddled her thighs, pinning her as I had the morning we'd met. Her gown had ridden up above her knees, and the skin of my calves sang as they pressed against her bare skin.

I placed my hands on either side of her shoulders and leaned over her.

"Siri. Wake up." I whispered.

And waited.

First, she smiled. A small sigh escaped her lips but I held myself back. As it was, I was probably breaking all the rules, waking her like this, like some sort of stalker. A knock on the door probably would have been more appropriate.

I started to reconsider.

Her eyes opened, blinking slowly, and then going wide. Silver reflecting the dim violet light coming from my own.

Oh well. Too late now.

"How did you get in?" she asked groggily. "Isn't the door keyed only to me and Auroreis?"

Even half-asleep, the girl was sharp.

"I have my ways," I said, grinning.

"I just bet you do. But, what are you doing here?" Open. I could feel it, all her emotions. The way she held herself exposed for me, the way her heart hid nothing. If I wanted her, she would accept me, all that I was, and all that I wasn't.

I swallowed.

"I wanted to talk to you before I left. I was on my way up here before, but Amber told me you'd already gone to bed. She told me what happened with you and the darkling."

She didn't like that. But not because she wanted him. Annoyed because she believed in him, his light. She didn't like it when I reminded her of his Dark side. I could feel it through the surge, her trust and loyalty. I imagined what it would be like to have that. To have all her trust.

All of her.

"And?" she ground out.

"And, I went back to my room to take a nap before I leave. I decided I would talk to you when I came back. Give you some time, and hopefully bring back some good news to cheer you up."

"But you changed your mind," she whispered, hope firing along the surge like lightning.

"I changed my mind," I whispered back, smiling down at her. "I promised you we would talk, so I'm here. To talk."

"To talk?" she asked, her lips curving upwards to mirror my own.

"Mmm, yes, to talk."

I couldn't wait any longer then. The surge was too strong, and telling me more than I needed to know. I leaned down and kissed her neck, her sigh tickling my ear. I nibbled my way down along her jaw, brushing lightly across her lips before retreating back up to gently kiss behind her ear, her body moving restlessly below mine as she moaned. Suddenly, she pulled my face back so our lips could meet again, and she opened to me, our emotions and energies twining together like kindred snakes.

I knew everything she was feeling, and with her, I knew that her feelings were the same as her thoughts. She was an open book to me, and I wanted to read every page a thousand times over. Again, the power and depth of her ability to love humbled me, shook me, and lured me in. She was strong, and yet so soft, so fragile. No boundaries protecting her from harm, her heart was completely unbound, unwarded.

I would have to protect her. No, I didn't have to. And she would never thank me for it. But I wanted to. Needed to.

Starting now. Starting with me.

I forced myself to rise up on my arms, to break the kiss, and stared down at her. Not a princess. My queen.

"That's it?" she teased. "Is that all you have to say?"

I laughed. She had no idea.

"You know very well it's not. I don't want to hide how I feel about you. But I also don't know where this can go," I said carefully. If I was going to do this, I needed to do it right. She needed to know all the risks. She needed to know me. We needed to take it slow. "I am half human. I'm lucky to even be here in Aeden, even more lucky to have become a Light Guard. You are a full fae; your father is practically an Ancient. You should be with someone of similar bloodlines. The Council is going to try to arrange a better pairing for you; it's inevitable."

"Let them try," she scoffed. She told me what her father had revealed to her that evening, how he and Vala believed she was the culmination of three bloodlines, possibly part of a prophecy that every faeling knew by heart. A girl who was fated to save the world. Or end it.

And she wanted me? I wondered if she really understood what it would mean if she was who and what they thought she was.

"There is no 'better pairing' for me. No one they could find that will be special enough. They'll never find anyone with ancestry like mine," she said. "I'm a prophecy, I'm special, unique. Which means I need a special sort of guy. A guy like you. Only you."

She pulled me down to her again, kissing me, captivating me with her open heart.

"They'll still try," I whispered in her ear, wanting to make sure she was all in. Fully committed.

The way I was.

"It won't matter," she said, kissing my neck. "I'm already yours."

After that, there were no words. Just lips and sighs and the surge. Finally, we broke apart. I fell back on the bed next to her. Not willing to let her go, I pulled her to me and she wound her leg around me, sighing one last time as I placed a chaste kiss upon her hair and we both dropped off to sleep.

My watch began to glow at 5am, the cyan light waking me slowly as it grew brighter and brighter. I opened my eyes and looked down at the girl in my arms, marveling at the prize I'd won.

I ran a hand over her hair, smoothing it, wishing I didn't have to go. But I had to. She needed me to leave, to travel back above below and find a cure for her mother, find a way to keep us all safe. To keep her safe. It was my prime directive now, to take care of this girl, this almost woman.

Carefully, I eased out of bed and gazed down at her sleeping form.

Missing her already, I walked away, out the door, back to my room.

It was a long, lonely walk.

Because I knew the truth now. I knew that Aeden would never be my true home. No one place ever would be again.

I had a new home now. No matter where I was, I would always be working my way back to her, her heart pulling me in like a compass towards true north.

Not homeward, but heartward. For all time.

ABOUT THE AUTHOR

Ellis Logan has been talking to fairies and writing stories since she was a little girl. She lives a quiet life with her family in New England, where she enjoys skiing, hiking, boxing and eating chocolate...always chocolate!

Follow Ellis on Facebook and Twitter at EllisLoganBooks

and

Join Ellis's mailing list at EllisLogan.com
to stay tuned for new releases, giveaways
and more!